3,00

MW01136849

WHISTLING TO CAIRO

OBIE YADGAR

outskirts
press

Whistling to Cairo
All Rights Reserved.
Copyright © 2022 Obie Yadgar
v2.0

This is a work of fiction. Names, characters, businesses, places, events, locales, and incidents are either the products of the author's imagination or used in a fictitious manner. Any resemblance to actual persons, living or dead, or actual events is purely coincidental.

The opinions expressed in this manuscript are solely the opinions of the author and do not represent the opinions or thoughts of the publisher. The author has represented and warranted full ownership and/or legal right to publish all the materials in this book.

This book may not be reproduced, transmitted, or stored in whole or in part by any means, including graphic, electronic, or mechanical without the express written consent of the publisher except in the case of brief quotations embodied in critical articles and reviews.

Outskirts Press, Inc.
http://www.outskirtspress.com

Paperback ISBN: 978-1-9772-4916-6

Cover Photo © 2022 www.gettyimages.com. All rights reserved - used with permission.

Author photo credit: Sadie Yadgar Hatzenbuhler

Outskirts Press and the "OP" logo are trademarks belonging to Outskirts Press, Inc.

PRINTED IN THE UNITED STATES OF AMERICA

For my girls
Judy, Sonja and Sadie

1

Margo was more than just love forever. She was a way of life. A once-in-a-lifetime experience. So how do you forget someone like that? It was a battle that Freddy kept on fighting. Because years after Margo walked out of his life he still thought about her. Maybe it was unfair to Gabrielle, her being his wife, but he couldn't help how he felt.

Gabrielle knew about Margo, of course, but she never talked about her. For all Freddy knew, she considered Margo a small blip in their marriage and locked her away out of sight. Until now, that is. With Chicago looming once again, Freddy had to admit to misreading Gabrielle all along. Margo was more than just a speck of dust in the wind, after all. She was a full blown storm as he prepared to leave for Chicago.

Freddy could see all that in the way Gabrielle behaved at the reception. It was obvious. She ignored him much of the night and instead melted on the dancefloor in Niko's arms. Niko was her co-star in the upcoming film *Ever Since We* Met, with production scheduled for the summer in Romania. Initially Freddy gave her the benefit of the doubt, that maybe she was trying to get to know her co-star. Gabrielle always prepared hard for her films. Then when Niko began exploring her neck with his lips and his hands roamed her bare back, seemingly without Gabrielle's objection, Freddy had enough of that and had to step in.

"Mind if I nibble on my wife myself, pal?" he said, tapping Niko on the shoulder.

"Yes, yes, sorry," Niko stuttered, releasing Gabrielle. "Sorry, I was not trying . . ."

"Sure you were not," Freddy cut him off, jerking Gabrielle into his arms. "Remember me, sugar?" he said. "Your friendly neighborhood husband."

The orchestra played "My Silent Love" and Savoy Hotel's ballroom glittered with an international guest list. Prince Hamid's reception honored his daughter Yasmine for her graduation from Oxford. The Jordanian prince and Freddy were longtime friends.

Freddy drew Gabrielle closer, but her body stiffened. "I don't feel like dancing," she hissed.

"Neither do I." Freddy tightened his grip.

Gabrielle's low-cut dress framed the curves of her breasts, the open back teasing Freddy's hungry hands. Strobe lights shot off sparkles from the diamond necklace Freddy brought her from Tel Aviv on his last concert tour of Eastern Europe and Israel.

"Look at me, Gabrielle," he said. The soft purple of her dress deepened her blue eyes. "This crazy behavior isn't getting us anywhere. We need to talk."

Gabrielle stopped fighting. "You're not worth talking to, mister fancy concert pianist."

"'Fancy concert pianist', oh, that's a new one. So what's my crime this time? I mean I commit so many."

"Your girlfriend."

"What girlfriend?"

"Waiting for you in Chicago." Gabrielle teared up.

"What gives you that idea?"

"I'm not stupid, Freddy."

"If you mean Margo, she was long ago and I've moved on." So much for hypocrisy, Freddy accused himself. "She has children, two of them, and I'm sure she's moved on, too."

"Oh please, don't give me that ridiculous . . ." Gabrielle freed herself. "You can go to hell, you know? I'm sure you can find your way."

Freddy wanted to say how well he knew the way, that he'd been to hell twice already: when he lost his parents, and then later when

Margo broke his heart and left him. Yes, he knew all about hell.

"Don't do this, Gabrielle," he pleaded. "It's starting to get a wee bit too much. Listen, when I return from Chicago, we can go to Vienna again, like the last time. I have a concert coming up there with the Vienna Philharmonic. We can make a nice little vacation out of it. I know Marguerite would love it, too. She did the last time we were there."

"Two of you can go together," Gabrielle snapped.

"I don't believe you said that." Freddy could see the immediate regret in her eyes. "Marguerite's your daughter, too, in case you need a reminder. Gabrielle, be sensible."

"I'm done listening," Gabrielle snapped. "Take your preaching someplace else." She then marched away, heading toward the circle where Niko held court.

2

George Paulik was as a big tycoon very much involved in the arts. To Freddy, also an old fox.

First came the phone calls. Then conversations over dinner in London, Munich, and Bucharest, closing with a handshake in Paris when Paulik finally managed to hook a reluctant Freddy into taking part in the 75th Anniversary celebration of Chicago Conservatory of Music, to be held on the Chicago campus and also at Orchestra Hall.

"The old feelings are bound to boil over with Margo living in Chicago," Freddy wrote to Rufus, his former instructor at the conservatory. Rufus and his wife Effie were also like parents to him. "You know I've refused to play in Chicago because of that. Just knowing Margo is nearby will be torture enough. I don't need the emotional turmoil, Ruf, especially with Gabrielle on the warpath," Freddy wrote.

Whether Paulik was aware of the history with Margo Freddy couldn't tell. Not a word from Paulik about any of that. Yet Freddy was sure the old fox knew exactly what he was doing when he finally said, "And you'll be home with friends and family again, son."

The thought of home was something that haunted Freddy much of his life. Just where exactly was his home? New Orleans of his childhood with his parents? The conservatory years in Chicago with Margo? Or London with Gabrielle? Where did he really belong?

Paulik promised total freedom for Freddy to handle his master classes and concert performances in any way he wished. "It's your show, my boy," he said.

"My boy is it now," Freddy grumbled under his breath as he packed his suitcase in the bedroom of his Kensington home. Gabrielle brushed her hair at the dresser. She hadn't said a word to Freddy since leaving Prince Hamid's reception.

"I asked you to come, Gabrielle," Freddy said, trying one more time to convince her. "You might surprise yourself and enjoy the trip."

Gabrielle stopped brushing and addressed him in the mirror. "And I said I needed time with the script for my film." She resumed brushing, and then stopped again. "And you need time with your girlfriend there."

"This is really getting tiring."

Gabrielle wasn't listening. "Burn her photograph, then. You have it on your desk like a shrine."

"My old friend Phil is in that photo, too, you know? The three of us. We were Kreutzer Trio. It was a publicity shot."

"I should burn the bloody photo."

"Like that will burn the past out of existence."

"No, but I'll have my husband back."

"I've been here all along."

"With your girlfriend's shadow hanging over us, yes," Gabrielle fought back. "Don't tell me that's not so, Freddy. Nobody's stupid here. I will not live in any woman's shadow. Not Gabrielle Mersenne."

Freddy finally had to get away from the constant barrage before Gabrielle drove him crazy. "So then I pretend Margo didn't happen?" He closed his suitcase. "Is that what you want to hear? Or maybe shut my eyes and the past will fly out the window, because you don't approve of the cast. Gabrielle, be reasonable. This isn't doing anybody any good."

"I don't care," Gabrielle shouted, slamming down her brush. The brush broke in half and the head flew half way across the bedroom. She burst into tears then, covering her face with her hands.

"Gabrielle, please." Freddy went over and held her quivering shoulders. "This isn't one of your film roles. Think of Marguerite."

Gabrielle jerked out of his grip, shouting again, "What can't you understand? I don't care about anything. About any of this. About anyone." She then stormed into the bathroom and slammed the door shut.

"Lately Gabrielle throws a tantrum if you sneeze the wrong way," Freddy wrote to Rufus. "It's getting out of hand and I can't wait to get away from her."

I-

3

The Photo was taken in front of the old water tower on Michigan Avenue the day Freddy formed Kreutzer Trio. In the photo, they stood facing the camera with sparkling smiles, arms around each other. All were first year students at Chicago Conservatory of Music. Freddy remembered thinking at the time how he would have given anything for Luke and Connie to be there, smiling and nodding their approval. They would be proud of their son, Freddy was sure.

He returned the photo to his desk and made himself another drink at the small corner bar. Luke's Steinway piano, now his, took up a big chunk out of the study, and a massive sound system took up a large corner across from it. Books and music lined the walls. Freddy referred to his study as his kingdom, where he often sat looking out into the cozy courtyard.

Freddy picked up the photo again and brushed a gentle hand over it, his heart yearning. How young they looked, and with hearts full of dreams. He remembered they went back and forth on a proper name for the trio, finally settling on Freddy's choice: Kreutzer Trio. "It's a name with strength and dignity," he said, and then, stretching his arms wide across, he added, "Kreutzer Trio with that mouth-watering hussy Margaret Kendrick, violin, that unfortunate soul, Philip Romney, cello and that legendary lover, Frederick Priestley, piano. It's magical, people. Watch out Beaux Arts Trio, here we come." All so long ago.

Freddy was still lost in his memories when Marguerite shuffled into the study clutching her teddy bear and rubbing sleep from her eyes. Freddy lifted her onto his lap and kissed her brow. "What's the matter, sugar, can't sleep?"

Marguerite shook her head no. "I miss you when you go away, Daddy," she whimpered.

"Oh, sugar, I miss you, too." Freddy squeezed her, his heart shredding. "I miss you a lot."

Suddenly he was back at the little house in New Orleans watching Luke and Connie get ready to leave for another gig. Now he knew what they must have felt leaving him. Freddy's baby sitter, a sweet little grandmother named Harriet, loved him, but she was not his mother, not Connie, and he missed his mother when she went away.

"I'll play Rachmaninoff's Third for my little Marguerite," Freddy promised. "How does that sound?"

"And send the audience whistling to Cairo?"

"Every time, sugar."

"How splendid, Daddy," Marguerite said, and put her arms around his neck. "I love you, Daddy. I love of you all of Mendelssohn's violin concerto."

"And I love you all of Beethoven's Emperor Concerto," Freddy said.

He kissed her little nose. "Young violinists need their proper sleep," he said, and took her back to bed.

If nothing else, Freddy knew, Gabrielle gave him Marguerite, and the little girl was the best thing that ever happened in his life.

4

The New Orleans of Freddy's childhood was a happy place, especially around dinner time, when conversation and laughter came with every course. Connie loved to cook and the fragrances that permeated the little house gave Freddy a sense of comfort and peace. Most of all, Freddy's New Orleans was music on a loop. Music day and night. And the music transported him to far off places. He heard sounds he never heard before. Melody and rhythm penetrated his soul and stirred all kinds of emotions in him.

Connie made the songs she sang hers, as if written for her. She wrapped "Early Autumn" and "Midnight Sun" in a package of silk and put a ribbon around it with "Do You Know What It Means to Miss New Orleans?"

Luke's piano laid a tapestry of luscious sounds around Connie's delicate voice. Luke was a Juilliard graduate and music poured out of him. Even at his young age, Freddy could feel his father's love for music, and especially for the piano. Luke could play George Gershwin and then easily slip into Robert Schumann. Or Brahms. He loved Debussy. When in a funk, he played Bach. Connie always said that Luke could have become a great concert pianist, but instead he chose her.

Connie always sang while she cooked. Her voice was warm like a fairytale and Freddy loved hearing it. Most of the time he didn't understand the lyrics, but that didn't matter. He wanted his mother's sweet voice and all the love that poured out of it.

Once over dinner Connie compared American standards by

George Gershwin, Cole Porter and other popular music legends to some of the art songs in the classical repertoire. They were just as good, she held.

Then she sang Franz Schubert's "Die Forelle"(The Trout), in German, the song Luke taught her, prompting Luke to slide behind the keyboard. From Schubert she segued into Irving Berlin's "Isn't This a Lovely Day?" Luke stayed with her, as if he knew the song was coming. Freddy loved both songs. Years later he thought Connie was right. Those great standards were just as good as Schubert's songs.

The night Freddy went to the nightclub With Luke and Connie his baby sitter was sick and there was no one else to watch him. Freddy was eight. Backstage Connie kissed his brow and asked if he had a request. "Isn't It Romantic," Freddy said. Connie sang the Rodgers and Hart classic around the house. Freddy stood backstage that night mesmerized by the show his parents put on. Connie floated through a treasure of romantic songs, Luke's piano building a lush cloud around her. During "Isn't It romantic" she looked over at Freddy standing off stage and flashed a smile. In the end she blew him a kiss. Through the years, Freddy marked that moment as one of the happiest in his life.

What dug up all the memories was the same tune now playing in Freddy's headphones on his flight to Chicago. He remembered Gabrielle asking him to play it for her the first time they met. He was flat broke at the time and worked as a cocktail pianist at a London hotel. Gabrielle sweetened her thanks with a kiss on his cheek. How things changed. When he left for Heathrow to catch his flight to Chicago, Gabrielle let him hug her, but no kiss on the cheek. "Good luck with everything," she said, and walked away. Change, indeed.

The flight attendant brought Freddy a drink and he sank back in his seat, wondering what kind of a reception to expect from Margo in Chicago. Although he did not have a recent photo of her, he knew Margo was still beautiful. Margo would always be beautiful, Freddy used to say, because her beauty came from within. The two of them shared a long past, he and Margo, a history, and they also might have built a future together, since their lives were intertwined like single notes sown into a full score. Might have. That was not to be, however. A long time ago, at Heathrow, Margo pushed out of his embrace and turned around and walked away.

When discussing plans over the phone with Margo to resurrect Kreutzer Trio for one performance for the celebration, Freddy heard no anger in her voice. They reminisced about the old days, about Phil and the rest of the gang. Margo laughed along with him. All seemed well, but Freddy doubted all was forgotten. They were best friends before becoming lovers, but since no longer lovers, perhaps being best friends was still a possibility.

Gabrielle would probably have something to say about that.

5

F reddy saw no other road in his life except for the one he chose long ago. Margo argued that their love for each other should come first. Besides, she couldn't take his gypsy life anymore. One day here, two days there, that wasn't what she wanted out of life. Margo wanted a family. Children. His children. She wanted a home for them close to her family. She wanted the children to be spoiled by their grandparents. They would have all of that in Chicago, she explained to Freddy, and from there he could launch his solo career, she added. Freddy argued such responsibility would tie him down and choke his chance of becoming the concert pianist that he wanted to be. "I need total freedom to give it all, Margo," he said. "Please try to understand. I made a promise to Luke, and to myself."

It was not to be. So long ago.

The flight attendant brought Freddy another drink. "A Jack Daniels with a quarter of note of water," she said, smiling. "That's a first for me."

Freddy remembered Margo saying the same things the night they met, when she walked into the cramped kitchen at that school party and forever changed his life. Her jeans and tight sweater framed a seductive body. Her hair rippled down her back like a shroud in ebony. Her eyes made him think of the blue waters off Santorini the time his parents took him there. Freddy's gaze stopped at Margo's mouth and he imagined his lips touching hers, kissing them, gently and long.

"You always look at girls like that?" Margo said, and stood facing him. "Kind of lusty."

"I look at girls, but not the way I'm looking at you, sugar," Freddy said, unable to take his eyes off of her.

"Sugar, that's a first for me."

"But it won't be the last."

"Well I'm glad to hear that." Margo looked around. "Anything else to drink besides beer and Coke?"

Freddy offered his drink.

"What is it?" Margo looked suspicious.

"Jack Daniels with a quarter note of water."

"Oh . . . That's another first for me."

"Jack Daniels on the rocks with a little water."

"Yes, I assumed something like that," she said. "From one musician to another."

"Aha!"

"I play the violin."

Freddy did a quick calculation in head and came up with a piano trio, with Phil playing cello.

Margo sipped his drink and made a sour face. "You always drink like this?"

"I'm from New Orleans," Freddy said, his mind photographing every part of Margo's face. Damn, he was falling in love her. No, not falling. He was in love with her.

"I should have asked do all you southern rebels drink like that?" Margo said, half way smiling.

"Oh sugar, I ain't no rebel. I Just play the piano."

"Yes, that you do," Margo said, beaming. "I heard you earlier tonight. You were incredible. How did you learn to play like that?"

"From my Daddy."

"He must have been quite a piano player, maybe another Artur Rubinstein."

Freddy's heart sank thinking about how much he missed his father. "No, he was just Luke Priestley. My father made the piano blossom like a bouquet of roses."

Margo took another sip from Freddy's drink and handed it back to him. She then started to say something but stopped.

"What?"

"I think I love you," she said, without hesitation. She looked into his eyes. "I feel so strange saying that. I love you. Yes."

Freddy brushed a hand across her lips and they parted, still moist from the drink. "I was just about ready to say the same thing to you."

"Well, do you?"

"I fell in love with you the moment I saw you earlier tonight, sugar." Freddy kissed her, gently. Margo let him. He kissed her again. "Stamped and sealed," he added, then.

That night Margo also stole Phil's heart, but Freddy claimed he saw her first and, best friend or not, Phil was obliged to put a bag over his head and waltz backwards. "And another thing," Freddy announced. "Margo plays violin. You play cello. Suddenly we have ourselves a trio."

"The broad's high society," Phil reminded him. "Those people are different. Their armpits don't smell."

Freddy laughed. "Next time I go around smelling armpits I'll keep that bit of wisdom in mind."

"And we wouldn't get past the butler, anyway," Phil kept on.

"No butler ever stopped me." Freddy put an arm around Phil. "I've picked that little flower for myself no matter where she grows."

6

The turbulence onboard the aircraft shook Freddy out of his thoughts. With little sleep for days, fatigue got the best of him. Closing his eyes didn't do any good either, because the memories flooded his head. He asked the flight attendant for a pot of coffee as his mind floated to Kreutzer Trio's first major concert at the conservatory.

Margo was nervous. Watching Freddy discuss the upcoming game between the Chicago Bears and the Green Bay Packers with a student stage hand, she announced, "Will someone tell me how this works?"

Phil picked up his cello, ready to go on stage. "What are you talking about, Margo?"

"Him," she said and pointed a thumb at Freddy.

Freddy winked and blew her a kiss.

Margo shook her head and smiled. "Here I am pacing like a caged animal," she announced, looking at Freddy first and then turning to Phil. "Hands sweating Niagara Falls, knees shaking like they're going to crumble. And here's this goofball, cool like a bwana." She turned to Freddy. "How can you be so disgustingly calm? Big audience out there."

Freddy put his cigar in an ashtray and loosened his finger. "Nothing to it, my luscious wild flower," he said. "I just go out there and play the piano, is what I do."

"Like it's that simple for the rest of us pedestrians," Margo snickered, her nerves showing in her voice. "I always feel like my slip is showing."

"Oh, Margo sugar, what heaven lies beneath that slip," Freddy chimed in with a lecherous smile.

Margo rolled her eyes again and tried to hide her smile. "You're impossible, Freddy."

Freddy chuckled and blew her a kiss. "But I love you, sugar."

Margo laughed and led the way onto the stage, violin tucked under her arm, Freddy following, and Phil third in line, Freddy whispering to Margo, "If only Schubert knew you, he'd have written a love serenade just on the way you waltz that exquisite tushy," and Margo, trying to choke her laughter, muttering, "Stop that, Freddy, you goof," and Phil grumbling, "Are we gonna play Schubert or keep fartin' around?"

The memories drained Freddy. He spent much of the night sitting at his desk pacing back and forth through his life. The goodbye scene with Margo at Heathrow kept coming back like a recurring dream. That was also the last time that he saw her.

He remembered Margo walking away from him, his throat tight, his lungs straining for air. Time dimmed the blinding glare from that image, but it did not wipe it off. Freddy lived with the pain all through the years. He wanted to see Margo again, even though he was not sure of the eruption inside him. Perhaps it was adding more pain to what Gabrielle was causing him already.

Margo was not at the airport to greet him, as expected, but only a conservatory representative waiting with a limousine to take him to his hotel downtown. Freddy telephoned Effie from the limo and promised to stop by later in the day. Effie scolded him for not staying at the house, but Freddie explained that it was to avoid creating turmoil in their lives. It was a year since he flew Rufus and Effie to London for Marguerite's birthday celebration.

He spoke with Phil, who was staying with his parents at their condo on Lakeshore Drive, and Phil told him to drop dead for not keeping in touch all those years. Phil also promised to write all kinds of nasty shit about him in the personal profile he was working on. Freddy rang off, laughing at Phil's permanently grumpy disposition.

The phone conversation with Marguerite from his hotel room lifted his spirit. She missed him, she said, and he knew she was being brave and holding back tears.

Gabrielle was ice when she came on the line. Not a word about Margo. She did manage to tell Freddy that she was having dinner with Niko, her co-star. Freddy was not pleased with the idea, especially considering Gabrielle's current frame of mind, but made no comment.

After Gabrielle rang off, Freddy poured himself a drink and stood looking out over the Chicago River and the high-rise buildings towering Navy Pier. Chicago seemed different, or was he the one different after so many years away from the city. Well, too much for his brain right now. He needed sleep. His first big concert at Orchestra Hall was two days away and he was grateful for the rest period. In the meantime he was scheduled for a pair of recitals at the conservatory as well as some master classes. And there was time to rehearse for his big concert.

He thought of calling Margo, but gave up on the idea. Instead he dreamed of her.

7

Margo once said that Freddy swept onto the concert stage like the second coming of Franz Liszt. She said he came on with such a distinct swagger that you could just imagine the sun rising from his keyboard. The truth was that he didn't even realize it himself, Margo said. There was nothing pretentious about it. Freddy just being Freddy. Wearing the spotlight like a halo.

Freddy was thinking about all that as he came onstage at Orchestra Hall to resounding applause. The newspapers proclaimed the event as the return of the prodigal son. Whatever, Freddy told himself. Anton Ritter, the Romanian guest conductor, followed a few steps behind. Freddy played the Prokofiev Second with Ritter in Bucharest the year before.

The first time Freddy played on this same stage he was hailed by critics as a rising star the classical music world should watch. He was in his last year at the conservatory. The moment was glorious for him, an awakening, when he finally understood what Luke meant when he said, "go out there and play the piano with your soul."

Margo reminded Freddy back then not to forget her when he became famous. Years later, with the name Frederick Priestley splashed all over major concert halls around the world, he did not forget Margo. Life tucked her deep inside him, life and his marriage to Gabrielle, but no, he did not forget Margo.

In the old days, he always felt her presence in the audience, waiting for him to send her whistling to Cairo. Then after the concert she always threw her arms around his neck backstage and kissed him passionately. She was in the audience now. Phil, Effie and Rufus were in the same row of seats. The guys in Rufus's jazz combo were there. Freddy knew some of his old friends from high school and conservatory were there, too.

Freddy vowed long ago to never play in Chicago, because Margo was there, because he knew seeing her again might kill him, and because he knew that after the concert he would have to return home to a turbulent life with Gabrielle. Yet here he was, playing in Chicago with Margo in the audience. Margo loved Rachmaninoff's Piano concerto No 3, some parts of it always bringing tears to her eyes. Freddy found it was a monster to play and dubbed it "The Gorgeous Monster." And here he was playing it for Margo. The Schumann A-Minor Piano Concerto, also a Margo favorite, was scheduled with the student orchestra at the conservatory in a few days.

After the applause quieted, Freddy adjusted the piano bench and sat down, arms at his side, his head lowered and eyes closed. Years earlier Margo wondered why he did that before every concert, whether playing solo or with Kreutzer Trio, and Freddy explained that it was his moment of truth, when he washed out everything else from his mind except for the music. "It was Luke's way," he said. "Like father like son."

Then Freddy lifted his head and winked at Ritter, who gave the downbeat to the orchestra and a few bars later Freddy entered with the piano.

When the Rachmaninoff exploded to a close, Freddy knew he had sent them whistling to Cairo. The audience shot to its feet bursting in resounding applause and bravos. Effie was beaming, one hand over her heart, and next to her, Rufus was nodding with a big smile. Phil was shouting bravos. Freddy thought he saw tears in Margo's eyes, but from that distance he couldn't be sure.

He saw his Marguerite applauding, and he heard her say, "Oh Daddy, what a splendid performance." Sitting with her, Luke and Connie were smiling. He heard them. Luke said, "That's how you play the piano, my little man," and Connie, a hand over her heart, in her Mae West imitation, saying, "Oh Freddy, honey, you sent them whistling to Cairo."

8

Margo played first violin in the string quartet. George Paulik played second violin, and a physician and a judge rounded out the group with viola and cello respectively. Except for Margo, all three were amateurs. The quartet got together on most Sundays at Paulik's mansion in Lake Forest, a wealthy city north of Chicago. In the summer, they played on the terrace overlooking the lush garden.

"I live for our quartet Sundays," Paulik said to Freddy. "Believe me, I'm in heaven." He then waved an arm across his estate. "I would give up all this for music."

Freddy knew what it meant to give up everything for music. "That's giving up a lot, Mr. Paulik."

"You should know," Margo struck.

The sting caught Freddy off guard. He threw her a cold smile.

Phil gave her a sour look but said nothing.

"What?" Margo played innocent.

Phil shook his head. Freddy kept silent.

They were at the post-concert reception at Paulik's mansion. Effie was tired and Rufus took her home after the concert. Following a whole lot of handshakes, introductions and media interviews, Freddy escaped to a quiet corner. Soon Margo and Phil joined him, and then Paulik.

"When the quartet plays on Sundays, it's always so sweet watching George and the other gentlemen get into the spirit of the music,"

Margo said, her tone softened. "Seeing them involved in the music is so inspiring."

"Kind of you to say that, my dear," Paulik said. "My musical spirit is lost without you guiding us."

"I learned how from a great musician a long time ago." Margo glanced at Freddy and then looked away. "He was a perfectionist and didn't settle for mediocre."

Freddy knew the reference. He led Kreutzer Trio. He was its musical mind. "Well, Margo has a way about her," he told Paulik. "A great fiddler and a disciplined musician."

Margo gave him a cold smile. "So nice of you to say that, *Frederick*." She stretched his full name like a rubber band.

Freddy never heard her call him by his full first name, stretched or otherwise. He let the sting go and said nothing.

Paulik was called away and Freddy, Margo and Phil were alone together for the first time since the concert.

"Your moment of truth was longer than usual," Margo said to Freddy. "I wondered."

"Too many oars in my head paddling in different directions," he said.

"You can get lost that way."

"Too late for that."

"Too late for a lot of things, *Frederick*." This time no rubber band. Just pure ice.

Phil made a sour face and kept quiet.

Again, Freddy let Margo's comment go. His eyes roamed her face. He saw beauty much deeper now, more captivating, like Brahms. Her hair was shorter, rippling down almost to her shoulders. Freddy thought he liked it better than before. The same eyes that always held him now had more depth. He felt they could read him better than they always did. Margo wore a black evening dress and a pearl necklace, revealing neck and shoulders the color of wheat after rain.

Freddy ached to touch her, to explore her neck and shoulders with his lips as he did long ago when Margo was his. She loved him then, and he worshipped her. But then Margo slipped away from him forever and that left him with a deep wound that never stopped hurting.

It was like being forbidden to play Brahms ever again. And he hurt for deceiving Gabrielle, because Margo was not long ago, really. Margo was now. Margo was in his thoughts almost every moment. He heard Luke say, "You embarrass me, Freddy. You're a married man."

Freddy's throat tightened and he forced his thoughts on Phil. His old friend and conservatory roommate was changed. He was a little pudgy now with thinner hair. Phil looked distinguished in his dark gray suite, but the single stud earring he wore confused the picture for Freddy.

When Phil noticed Freddy eyeing the earring, he tapped a finger on it and frowned. "Have to wear the damn thing for a month. Lost a bet with my boys."

"Lost something, old buddy," Freddy snickered.

"That's so sweet," Margo cooed, touching the earring, her mood changed.

"He looks like Mister Clean in his Sunday suit, Margo."

"He does, doesn't he?"

"Stick him in a bottle and take him home."

"Put him on the cover of your new recording," Margo shot back, her cold eyes like knives.

Freddy shook his head in frustration. "Between shots of Schumann and Grieg," he played along.

"I'd buy the CD just for the cover," Margo chuckled.

"You morons don't know class when you see it," Phil stepped in, laughing.

Nearby in a circle of conservatory donors, Sheila Brentwood laughed, drawing Phil's attention. He beamed.

"You like Sheila, don't you?" Margo turned to him.

Phil nodded yes. "Rumors about her true?"

Margo didn't like the specter of Sheila around Freddy, and took comfort knowing Phil was interested in her. "She's married twice," Margo said, "and rumor has it she spits out men like cherry pits."

"Hmmm." Phil nodded and kept his eye on Sheila. She turned and smiled at him.

"But I'm skeptical about the rumors," Margo added. "That's unfair to Sheila."

Sheila was a powerful voice on the conservatory board.

"I remember her from the conservatory days." Freddy studied her from the distance. "Played the flute, I think."

"Flute, yes," Phil said. "She was a dish."

"All the guys had the hots for her," Freddy said.

"You the most, probably," Margo fired.

She took too many shots at Freddy and he was getting tired of ignoring them. "Okay, Margo," he said, "I've planned a weekend getaway with Sheila, with Phil's okay."

"I hope you have a good time," said Margo.

Phil stepped in to cut the sniping. "Sheila said she loves your boutique, Margo. *Swan*, is it? On Michigan Avenue."

"I hear it's a lovely shop," Freddy said to Margo. "You always did have good taste."

"You mean you haven't seen little Margo's discount store for the rich?" Phil joked. "You sneeze in *Swan* and it costs you a thousand bucks."

"Yes, well, *Swan* doesn't cater to peasants," Margo declared. "Sheila's one of my best customers."

"Knows how to dress, for sure," Phil said. "It's nice. Looks like a movie star."

Margo turned to Freddy with a blow. "Your wife is a movie star. You should stop in and pick up a few items for her."

If Margo continued to goad Freddy into a fight, he did not bite. He was too tired of fighting. No thanks. Gabrielle was a big enough fight already and another one with a jilted woman he didn't need.

"I'll be sure to do that," he said to Margo, and shuffled away to the bar for a drink.

9

Just the thought of Margo married to someone else, sharing his bed, having his children, just that image was enough to torture Freddy.

"What did you expect?" Rufus wrote. "What did you think was going to happen? That girl loved you. Wanted to make a life with you. And you were nuts about her. But she was sacrificed."

"I did what I had to do," Freddy wrote, without meaning to sound defiant. "It was a painful decision to make. Almost killed me. But . . . Sometimes I have to wonder if it was all worth losing the only woman I have truly loved in my life."

"Only you would know the answer to that, boy. You made your choice and you have to live with it."

"That I lost Margo to be where I am now?"

"We'll never know now, will we?" Rufus wrote. "Doesn't matter. You deal with it either way."

When Freddy heard about Howard's death, he tried calling Margo and froze every time. Just hearing her voice was enough to break him. He tried writing, but somehow his fountain pen failed to make a mark on the paper.

Howard knew Margo long before Freddy came along. The Lang and Kendrick families went back several generations in Chicago. Margo's family, the Kendricks, were in auto parts manufacturing and Howard's in clothing. *Swan* was Margo's anniversary gift from Howard: a sophisticated Michigan Avenue boutique created in her image. Howard worshipped Margo. For a short time in the old days he was even part of the gang, often talking about becoming Kreutzer Trio's agent and business manager after graduation from Northwestern, but his family quashed that notion and Howard joined the family business.

George Paulik knew all that, and he also knew Freddy's history. Rufus always said George Paulik knew everything. For his turn, Paulik wanted famous graduates for the 75th Anniversary. Frederick Priestley was the biggest prize. Not only was he a celebrated concert pianist, but also a highly regarded jazz musician.

"It's grand seeing you in your hometown, son," Paulik told Freddy in the dressing room after the Rachmaninoff concert. Freddy reminded him that he was born in New Orleans. Not about to be checked, Paulik laughed and jokingly said, "And what's more, son, we'll make you famous."

Freddy reminded Paulik of the Jascha Heifetz story: when Samuel Goldwin wanted him for a movie and thought his price tag too high. "Money isn't everything, Mister Heifetz," Goldwin reportedly is known to have said. "I can make you famous."

When Freddy relayed his conversation with Paulik to Phil and Margo at the reception, Phil ignored it. "So what was Sheila doing in your dressing room all alone?"

"Just a courtesy call." Freddy frowned. "What do you think she was doing there?"

"Sharpening her claws," Margo hissed.

"Sorry, sugar, but Sheila's Phil's honey."

"And you keep your paws off her, old buddy," Phil threatened.

"You have my word on it." Freddy held up a hand and then, joking, said, "Maybe I can find me another wild woman."

Margo's head snapped around and she drilled Freddy with an icy look. "And what will your wife say, or is that routine with international stars?"

"Smash her drink against the goddamn wall and then go out partying with her movie buddies. Is that what you want to hear?"

"Will you two cork it?" Phil snapped, irritated at the jousting. "This is a reunion and we're supposed to hug and kiss."

"Margo's hormones are in the venom cycle."

"Why is it always venom with women and just a loud bark with men?" Margo shot back.

"I'm sure you have an answer for that." Freddy put up his hands. "I'm tired, Margo, and you have my surrender. Stand me up against the wall and shoot me. That should make you happy."

Margo tried to say something, but shook her head instead and kept silent.

The waiter brought Freddy's drink, Jack Daniels on the rocks with a hint of water and Freddy held up his glass. "To the different roads taken."

"And all the twists and turns," Phil followed.

They waited for Margo. She took her time before adding, "Sure, why not?"

Margo needed to check on the children and excused herself. Freddy and Phil watched her slink off.

"I suppose you know little Margo still loves you," Phil said, "but we both know you don't deserve her."

"I know I don't." Freddy studied his drink.

"Sorry, Freddy, that didn't come out right."

"No, you're right. I've said that to myself over and over again. No, I don't deserve her. Damn, I've never stopped loving her."

Freddy looked around the room. A grand piano sat in one corner. In the old days he didn't need an invitation to sit at the keyboard and blast away with Brahms Hungarian dances. Not now, though. Gabrielle and Margo sapped his energy. Squeezed him like a lemon. Took every bit of life out of him. He turned to Phil and said, "You don't fall in and out of love with Margo like you're on a weekend visit."

"Does Gabrielle know all this?

"I think women have an extra sense for smelling smoke," Freddy said.

"Not good."

"No, and I don't know what to do. Living with Gabrielle is like fighting a typhoon."

Across the room, George Paulik called for attention. He spoke about the anniversary celebration as well as some of the conservatory expansion plans. He outlined some of the programming, and thanked Freddy especially for his contribution to the event by holding master classes as well giving recitals.

It all sounded strange to Freddy. The gang was back in Chicago and getting ready to walk the conservatory hallways and to make music together again. Paulik was making announcements that reminded Freddy of the loudspeakers crackling in the hallways with student instructions and conservatory news events. The three of them were back together again, he, Phil and Margo, yet he felt a distance among them. It was like the old times again, and yet it was not.

Rufus always said that life didn't make any sense. No argument from Freddy.

10

Freddy convinced Margo and Phil to help resurrect Kreutzer Trio for one more concert only. The three were graduates of the conservatory, after all, and how great it would look for the institution, he reasoned. In the end Margo and Phil agreed, although reluctantly.

"I should kill you for suckering us into the trio thing," Margo told Freddy earlier at the reception. "I'm not sure if I'm up to it. I can still play, but it's hard going back."

"Going back to what, Margo?" Freddy said. "You're a musician, violinist, and you go out there and play. Don't think it. Feel it. Have fun."

"Hell, if all fails, we'll just sit there and pluck the strings," Phil said.

"Also remember, Margo, one look at you and the audience will hunger for more of you," Freddy kept on.

"Like watching a strip tease," Phil chimed in.

"Oh please," Margo laughed, "won't that make Paulik and the old fogies on the board happy."

"Give the critics something to write about," Phil snickered.

"You know what Rossini called criticism," Freddy said. "The world's most useless occupation."

"Well, Rossini's not here," Margo complained.

"Okay, then, how about this one," Freddy said. "This critic dies and there's no money to bury him. His friends ask a composer for a contribution toward the burial. 'What's my share?' he asks. 'Thirty krone, maestro,' they say, and he says, 'Here's sixty krone, burry two critics.'"

They laughed together and Freddy loved seeing it after all the years. "Come on guys, we had fun making music in the old days," he said. "Just one more Kreutzer Trio concert for the road."

"I'll feel naked in front all those people," Margo complained, shivering.

"But they'll also get their jollies watching you," Freddy said. "Two for the price of one."

"We're back at that again, I see," Margo chuckled. "I don't know how I ever put up with you juveniles."

"We'll have to lean on you, old buddy," Phil said, and Margo added, "We always did and Freddy made us shine."

11

Connie's sound was a mix of June Christy's sultry tone and Lee Wiley's smokey voice. Somewhere in there. She was warm, intimate, even sexy, a picture postcard of a cabaret singer. As for Luke, his piano was so introspective and so seductive that you could almost feel his soul rising from the keyboard. Connie and Luke were made for each other as musicians, a perfect matching of voice and piano.

Freddy was reminiscing with Rufus and Effie over coffee in Effie's kitchen. Following Paulik's post-concert reception, Freddy sat in with Rufus's quartet at the Jazz Notebook on the south side until close. Then on to Rufus and Effie's for bacon and eggs and coffee. It was past midnight and fatigue was catching up with Freddy. Still, he couldn't tear himself away from Effie's coffee served with all the memories. He had no concert scheduled that day, but he was looking at several master classes at the conservatory.

"We dropped in the club in New Orleans one night to hear them," Effie recalled. "Connie was pregnant with you, Freddy honey. It was the night she sang 'Sophisticated Lady' and I almost fell out of my chair. Never heard anyone sing it like that. Remember, Rufus?"

Rufus nodded, and thought. "Celestial is what Luke called it. That man sure had a way with words."

Effie brought over a fresh pot of coffee and filled the cups. "Freddy honey, celestial is what it was. What beautiful singing."

"And Luke's piano," followed Rufus. "Oh man, he stayed with

Connie, under her, around her, throwing rose pedals in her path. Man, that cat had beautiful technique. Great style. Sophisticated. Pure class. And he played with so much love."

"Luke always told me not to bang on the piano like it was a garbage can, but to play as if making love to a beautiful woman," Freddy said. "I was too young and didn't understand what exactly he meant. Luke said to remember those words and that someday I'll understand."

Rufus sipped his coffee and nodded his approval. "I hear a lot of Luke and Connie in you," he said to Freddy. "It's that passion and that soul in your playing that reminds me of Luke. You got that from him, for sure. From your parents. I heard it the first time you came into my class for your initial audition."

That day Freddy set out to conquer and conquer he did. He dazzled his professors at the conservatory. One asked him to play anything he wanted and Freddy proceeded to play the Bach Goldberg Variations. It didn't take the professor long to stop him. "Young man," he said, "maybe you can teach me instead of having it the other way around."

Rufus said what he didn't expect at the audition was a brilliant musical tour from Bach to Mozart, Beethoven to Brahms, Chopin to Schumann, Debussy to Rachmaninoff, all then wrapped up with a ribbon of Bud Powell, Bill Evens, Oscar Peterson and John Coltrane. Freddy mesmerized him, Rufus recalled. "Where did you learn to play like this at your age?" he asked Freddy.

"First from my Daddy," Freddy said, "and then I kept on studying and playing."

"Who was your daddy?"

"Luke Priestley. My father was a pianist down in New Orleans. I was born there."

Rufus remembered thinking for a moment and then saying, "You're Luke's boy? Luke and Connie's?"

"Yes, sir. Did you know my parents?"

"I surely did," Rufus said. "Knew them pretty good."

Later in the day after the audition Rufus took Freddy home to meet Effie. They had dinner and then talked music late into the night.

Rufus left the kitchen and then returned with a box of Montecristo cigars Freddy sent him. They both lit up. Effie gave them another refill of the coffee.

Freddy had several cups already, but who could resist Effie's coffee in Effie's kitchen? He watched her with the coffee pot, thinking how much he loved her.

"Music was Luke's passion," Freddy said, and sipped his coffee. "Music and his piano. He lived for them. Looks like he passed all that to me."

"And your mama and daddy were so happy together, Freddy honey, more than any people I've known," Effie said.

Rufus then regarded Freddy. "Are you happy, boy?"

The question caught Freddy by surprise. All night there was no mention of his current life, and nothing about Gabrielle. Freddy made a sour face and tossed a dismissive hand in the air.

Rufus frowned. "How come you never say in your letters?"

What, Freddy wanted to say, that Gabrielle's affair with the *Algerian Dawn* film director doomed their marriage? Things were sour between them already and that the affair was the big turning point in how he felt about his marriage.

"Beautiful woman, Gabrielle," Effie said, and looked at Rufus as if expecting a response.

Rufus sipped his coffee and thought. "Saw her in that movie with the . . . what was it?"

"*Algerian Dawn*, I think you mean," Freddy said.

Freddy remembered arguing with Gabrielle against accepting the leading role in the movie. The script was crap, he warned. Some Algerian Mata Hari in sordid bedroom scenes with a French Foreign Legion officer. What the hell? Gabrielle defied him and made the film anyway. *Algerian Dawn* was a financial blockbuster. After all, Gabrielle had enough nude and love making scenes in it to pack movie houses around the world. The film was an artistic disaster, though. The critics were particularly cruel, and they questioned why a beautiful and talented actor lowered herself into a movie sewer. Gabrielle took it hard. So did her career.

"I'm surprised you remember the movie, Ruf?" Freddy said.

"All them fornicating parts. Who can forget? Maybe called acting, but it was damn embarrassing to watch, don't you think, Effie?"

She agreed, nodding. "Awful shame," she said.

Effie poured more coffee. Freddy thought about sleep and then his class. He expected a tough day.

"Sometimes Gabrielle confuses acting with reality," Freddy said. Not that he experienced that reality lately, he told himself. It was months since they slept together. "I think Marguerite is the only reason we're together," he said.

"I'm so sad for you, honey." Effie reached over and touched his cheek. A loving touch. "What's happening would break your mama's heart."

Freddy turned her hand and kissed her palm. "I know, sweetheart."

Freddy checked his watch again. Now three in the morning. He was slowly sinking from fatigue. After his master class he planned to take Margo out for a drive and then to dinner.

"I'll stop by the club later tonight and bring Missy along," Freddy said to Rufus. "We can make it like the old times."

Rufus always addressed Margo as Missy. Margo took a few classes from him at the conservatory, but she was the first to admit that she wasn't exactly Stephan Grappelli, the legendary jazz violinist.

"Hadn't seen Missy for a long time until the concert," Rufus said. "Beautiful woman that one. You shouldn't have let her go, boy."

"I shouldn't have done a lot of things, Ruf."

"So now Missy's a widow and you're still married."

"That seems to be the case."

Rufus drank his coffee and thought.

"What are you saying, Ruf?"

"I'm saying not to do anything stupid, boy."

No, nothing stupid, Freddy told himself. He did enough stupid in his life already. No more. At least he hoped. "I hurt Margo once, Ruf, and I don't plan a repeat. And I don't want to hurt Gabrielle."

Effie returned to the kitchen. "Freddy honey, it's late. I've made your bed in your old room."

"Effie's right, son," Rufus followed. "Don't want you on the roads when you're ready to pass out."

It felt like old times for Freddy, when he often spent the night. He felt warm and comfortable at Effie's. There was peace in the house, and he was loved once again by his parents. Yes, Effie and Ruf were parents to him.

Freddy nodded okay and then wrapped his arms around Effie. "I love you, sweetheart" he said. "You are my Mama."

12

So this is how the idea started.

Freddy was back from a series of concerts in the U.S. and South America. Paulik was still trying to nail Freddy for the conservatory celebration. With Gabrielle staying at their Paris apartment for some television appearances, Freddy and Marguerite were together for the weekend. At a little brasserie in Kensington Freddy started telling Marguerite about his experience hitchhiking from Chicago to Los Angeles the summer after graduation from the conservatory.

Marguerite was excited and kept asking him to tell her more. Finally she said, "Oh, Daddy, can we hitchhike together across the United States?"

He should have expected something like that, because Marguerite had his adventurous spirit. "Well, sugar, hitchhiking is a tough act," he said, "but we can drive across America together."

"Oh, Daddy." Marguerite beamed.

"In a red Camaro," Freddy added, just as excited as Marguerite. "Convertible. With the top down. Zooming across the U.S.A."

"That is splendid. Oh, Daddy, I'm so excited."

"So am I, sugar," Freddy said, not sure what he got himself into. Cross-country drive with a ten-year-old? What was he thinking? What was he supposed to do? There was no Nannie or Gabrielle to take care of her needs. Lord help him. But then it took another few moments for joy to overcome trepidation. Suddenly he found himself as excited as Marguerite and couldn't wait until the coming summer.

"Oh Daddy, do you promise?"

Freddy held up a hand as a promise. He called Gabrielle. She thought it a good idea, especially since she was going to be on location in Romania during the time they were playing across America.

So it was settled: father and daughter, two cavaliers zooming down America's highways. In the meantime, the weekend was theirs and they planned to spend it with aplomb, or something like that, Freddy told himself. They went to the cinema, visited the Tate Museum, feasted on hamburgers and French Fries, and milk shakes. Marguerite continued to talk about the cross-country trip and was full of questions. Freddy looked for creative roadmaps to follow and memorable places for them to see. He loved every moment spent with his excited little girl.

All that brought back memories of his excitement when he thought up the hitchhiking idea the summer after his graduation. He dropped the bomb on Margo and asked her to go along with him. And what a bomb it was.

"Whatever gave you that crazy idea, Freddy?" Margo barked. "Are you insane?"

"Nope. Sane as Abe Lincoln on a five-dollar bill."

"But why? What do you expect to gain? And drag me along."

"Adventure. You and me together meeting America."

"And what do you think my parents will say? And I'm not sure I want to go either like some female Sancho Panza. Get real, Freddy."

"I'm tired of real," Freddy suddenly exploded. "Too much real in my life, Margo. I'm sick of it."

"Okay, okay, we'll talk about it later." Margo wrapped his arms around her waist and placed a small kiss on the corner of his mouth.

Looking back, Freddy thought how easily Margo calmed him down. Mellowed him.

Margo was right, though. Her father refused to hear another word about Freddy's adventure. So did her mother. Not a word.

"I suppose there's no use trying to convince a hard-headed idiot like you not to do something once you set your mind to it." Margo was trying everything to dissuade Freddy. "No, of course, not. And I suppose you're not going to think about me worrying to death about you. Sure, why should you?"

But Freddy had made up his mind.

Effie was against it, too, saying she'd worry to death about him. Rufus was the only one who told Freddy to go out there and learn about the world. Rufus also said to play the piano whenever and wherever possible.

In the end, Freddy defied Margo and took off on his adventure. He learned some things about the world, only to fly back in September to face Margo's anger.

"Don't you ever do a crazy thing like that again," she cried, burying herself in his arms.

No, never again, Freddy promised. In the end he did something worse, which led to Margo's teary goodbye on a rainy Sunday at Heathrow as they parted.

Sometimes in the quiet hours, memories of that summer on the road trickled back and washed away the present conflicts in Freddy's life. They did in his hotel room as he lathered to shave — he still had Luke's Simpsons shave brush, although he had it re-knotted, and his father's restored Wade & Butcher straight razor. Couple hours of sleep were all he managed at Effie's and then drove back to his hotel. He was worn out and faced a long day, but his memories remedied concerns about the hours ahead.

Leaving the shelter of the conservatory that summer long ago, he saw the other side of the world, along the way working as farmhand, waiter, bartender, and he played piano in clubs and retirement homes. Finally, after spending two weeks in Los Angeles playing piano wherever he could, Freddy flew back to Chicago in the first week of September. So long ago.

Freddy finished his shave and ordered breakfast. He also called Marguerite in London. She came on the line excited about the cross-country trip. "Oh, Daddy-Daddy," she bubbled in her British accent that Freddy loved, "we shall soar down the highways of America and blast country music on the radio."

For heaven's sake, sometimes Marguerite surprised him. "Country music, sugar? Since when?"

"My good man," Marguerite announced, now in her British

royal accent, "how else would two free spirits soar down America's highways?"

"Pardon me, *Her Royalness*, how else, indeed?" Freddy laughed, and could hear Marguerite laughing with him. Then she was quiet. "What is it, sugar?"

"I wish Mummy could come on the road with us," she confessed.

Freddy heard little tears in her eyes. "So do I, sugar," he said, not sure Gabrielle cared for her hair blowing in the wind across American highways. Nor did he think she had the patience for sight-seeing. Besides, Gabrielle was going to Romania to make a movie.

When Freddy asked to speak with Gabrielle, Nanny said Madame was at the Paris apartment. He should not be surprised, Freddy reminded himself. Gabrielle was angry with him and escaping to Paris was her way of punishing him. Escape to the Paris apartment meant a marathon of drinking parties and who knew what else with her cronies and the hangers-on. In time Freddy gave up arguing with her about her lifestyle there. At least, whenever Gabrielle went crazy, she made sure it was as far away from Marguerite as possible.

Marguerite came back on the line. "Mummy will be filming in Romania, I forgot," she said. "Then just the two of us in the red Camaro, Daddy. How splendid."

"My Marguerite and me going out and learning about the world," Freddy said, his eyes filling with dew. If he could only drop everything and fly back to London just to hold his little girl.

Freddy considered calling Gabrielle at the Paris apartment, but gave up on the idea. Not sure she would answer the phone, or if she did, she'd probably breath fire into his ear and then hang up. Or Gabrielle would be cool and calm and then ask how his girlfriend is doing. What difference did it make? He wasn't up to an argument with a beautiful but explosive French actor, who happened to be his wife, and who was on the warpath.

13

The 1969 model Camaro was Freddy's high school graduation gift. It was a used Indy pace car replica, convertible, in white with red stripes, and rear spoiler. With low mileage, pristine body and muscular engine, the Camaro drove like Red Garland's hard bop piano, Freddy told Margo.

The way Uncle Dennis put it: that if Freddy was going to drive, it might as well be in a sweet chariot. And he came through. Dennis Priestley, Luke's older brother, left New Orleans for Chicago after their parents passed away and eventually opened an automobile dealership in the city. He had no children of his own and treated his nephew like a son. Freddy lived with him until moving into conservatory dorms.

Freddy named the Camaro Aurore, because the name popped into his head the first time he slid behind the wheel. It just came out of nowhere and bang. The morning after he met Margo at that party thrown by one of the conservatory kids, it was a Saturday and Freddy drove his Aurore to the big house in Wilmette. By the time he left with Margo to go for a drive, he already dazzled her parents with his southern charm.

"I didn't lay it on too thick, did I?" Freddy said, opening the car door for Margo.

"Don't worry," she said, splashing herself in the front seat, "they'll have you over for dinner before you can say Jambalaya."

"Maybe I can ask them for your hand, sugar."

"And I wouldn't be surprised at all if they said yes. They're already in love with you." Margo touched the dashboard and flashed an impressed smile. "But don't you think maybe we're just a little too young for that?"

"I've already decided you're the love of my life, sugar, but I can wait till after the finals."

Margo laughed. "How you do carry on, Mister Priestley."

It was a warm spring day and Freddy felt the world was painted in laughter. He loved the way Margo splashed herself in the front seat, as if she belonged there. Driving off, he said, "Even Aurore adores you, beautiful Margo."

"Who's Aurore?"

"You are in Aurore."

Margo regarded him. "Oh, the car. It has a name?"

"Named after Chopin's lover Gorge Sand, which was pen name for Amantine Lucile Aurore Dupin, later Dudevant." Freddy turned on the radio: a Vivaldi violin concerto. "Chopin met her at his friend Liszt's salon at the Hotel de France in Paris. Sand often dressed butch and smoked cigars." Freddy flipped his brow and made a lecherous face. "Now that's my kind of a woman."

"You like women who look butch and smoke cigars?"

"For all I know, they can be mud wrestlers as long as they look like you," Freddy said, and winked.

"Good to know." Margo blew out a breath. "Now tell me how you know all this about Chopin and George Sand."

"I know a lot of things."

"And cocky, too," Margo humored him, "and you've named your car Aurore."

"I name everything I own that means something to me. It brings it to life." Freddy gunned the engine. "Ooooooh, that sounds sweet."

Margo smiled at his little-boy excitement. "For a guy, I thought you might have named the car, oh, I don't know, Lulu May, or Sweet Baby, or some other macho name."

"Careful, sister, Aurore is listening."

"Oh, sorry."

At a stoplight, Freddy lit a cigar. "I'm sorry, do you mind?" he asked.

Margo, surprised at the cigar, shook her head no.

Freddy took a big puff as the light turned green. He gunned the engine and the car flew. "My piano at Uncle Dennis's house is Clara," he said.

"After Clara Wieck Schumann, I suppose."

"Robert Schumann's wife, yes. Hell of a pianist, apparently, and she wrote some good tunes, too."

Margo studied Freddy's profile.

"What?" he said.

"You're beautiful, you know?" Margo said. "A young Frantz Liszt, with that flowing gold mane of yours."

"Shucks, Margo, you make me blush, but thank you."

"You're welcome."

"You know, Persians have a saying — 'You're looking at me with beautiful eyes.' At least I think that's what they say."

"That's so sweet, Freddy, thank you," Margo said. "Now tell me, why you always name things after women?"

Freddy took another long puff from his cigar. "I thought of naming my piano at Uncle Denis's house Big Bruce, but somehow I couldn't see that inspiring a Chopin ballad."

Margo laughed and a lock of her hair slipped over her eye. "Tell me more about Chopin."

"Initially Chopin thought George Sand wasn't exactly the coolest looking chick in the neighborhood."

"I hope you didn't think that about me."

"I love everything about you." Freddy brushed the persistent lock of her hair from her eye again. "When I saw you last night, everything stopped for me."

"God, such a romantic." Margo rubbed her elbow — a habit Freddy discovered she had whenever she pondered something. "Why do I feel you're like a character in a novel?"

Freddy brushed her lips with the back of his hand. How soft. He could almost taste them. "Oh sugar, when I'm with you, I couldn't be any more real," he said.

The sun warmed the cool breeze. Mozart played on the radio and then Chopin and then Brahms.

"If there is such a thing as a state of perfection, of bliss, this is it for me," Freddy said.

"I feel like a queen riding in Aurore," Margo followed.

Freddy gunned the engine. "Enough power to field a squadron of chariots for your majesty," he said.

At a traffic light, he kissed her, and Margo kissed him back. He felt intoxicated.

They stopped for lunch. They talked.

"I have an army for a family," Margo said, "and we're so normal you can serve us with a plate of fried chicken and mashed potatoes."

"Nothing normal about you, sugar." Freddy studied Margo's face, the chiseled feature, the penetrating eyes, the sensual mouth. He wanted just to sit there and lose himself in Margo.

Margo frowned. "I think that's a compliment?"

"A high compliment in your case."

"Well, that's good to know." Margo reached over and Freddy took her hand. "Now tell me about Frederick Priestley, the hotshot pianist," she said.

"The only thing not musical in my little family was brushing teeth at bedtime," Freddy said, "but if I knew my father, sooner or later he would have come up with a musical arrangement just for that."

"Your dad sounds cool," Margo said.

Freddy nodded, not sure how to respond. "My parents, Luke and Connie, yes, they were cool," he said, his eyes filling with dew. "They had so much love in them, and they loved me. Then one day they became just a memory."

Margo's face froze.

"My parents were killed in a car crash. Drunk driver."

"Oh God." Margo reached over again and Freddy took her hands. "Oh God, I'm so sorry, Freddy," she said, her eyes tearing up.

Freddy flipped a brow. "I was ten years old."

"Oh God, Freddy, you don't have to . . ."

"That's all right. I should tell you about my life." He paused and looked away for a moment. "Suddenly I couldn't touch them anymore. Or to be held by them. Sung to by Mom. No more playing piano duets with Luke. We used to do that a lot, you know?"

Freddy told Margo a lot more about his parents and she listened intently. He found her easy to talk to. In the end, Margo wiped her tears and with the same hand reached over and wiped his.

"Luke and Connie, your parents, will always be there with you, don't you know that?" she said.

"I know in my heart and in my head." Freddy held her hand and kissed it. "I just wish I could have them in my arms, too."

Later Margo wondered what he wanted most in life. Freddy pondered a moment. "To be a concert pianist. I know Luke would have wanted me to. And Mom. Both of them. Yup. Float onto the concert stage and just play the piano. I want that dream, Margo, and I'll do anything for it."

"And you'll have it, Freddy," Margo said, "because I feel nothing will stand in your way."

"But I'm not finished with your question."

"Oh?"

"And I want you, Margo. More than anything. You and my piano."

Through the years Freddy always remembered that warm and sunny day in Aurore with Margo. Long after he was married to Gabrielle, he found himself going back to Margo's image splashed in the front seat in the Camaro. Most of all, he remembered their first kiss, at the stoplight. He still tasted it. He remembered once Gabrielle asked him, "Penny for your thoughts." He shrugged and gave her some evasive response.

Freddy thought he was unfair to Gabrielle for entertaining such thoughts about Margo. He felt guilty. Yet how could he forget the moments spent with Margo that meant so much to him? Looking at his life, Margo was his first love and she left her signature on his heart. Years later and that signature still had not faded.

14

reddy parked in front of Margo's house in pouring rain, a battle raging inside him: Margo, Gabrielle, memories, his life teetering on the edge. Again he questioned his decision to come to Chicago, because he walked right into a firestorm. It was a while before he noticed Margo standing in the doorway. He shut off the engine and ran up the walkway.

"What were you doing out there, praying?" Margo said, closing the door behind them.

She took his wet coat and gave him a towel to dry. Freddy nodded his thanks and then, looking around, said, "Why did I have the feeling your home would look something like this?"

Margo's house blended rich wood with exquisite Persian carpets, and the Impressionist paintings dressing the walls threw a warm sheen over everything. An elaborate sound system took up one corner and a grand piano another.

"What about my house?" she said.

"Warm and beautiful like you." Freddy swept an arm across. "Nothing like my little house in London. This is pure luxury. My study has character, though, I admit, or I should say, is cured in a rich bouquet of cigar and pipe smoke, bourbon and old books. Drives Gabrielle crazy. Calls me 'The Steinway Barbarian.'"

Margo laughed. "I know all about places like that."

"Our little flat in London? It had character."

"The smell from your so-called character got all over my clothes,

Freddy."

"But it was our special place."

"Yes, it was," Margo whispered.

They looked at each other with longing smiles.

"Well, ready for a drive?" Freddy said. "We'll put the top down and blast the radio clear to Wisconsin."

"For heaven's sake, Freddy, it's pouring rain."

"Well then, we won't put the bloody top down. Maybe we can stop at that little café where we went on our first chariot ride. Remember? If the place is still there."

Margo nodded. "I've been there for lunch." She then looked away. "Once or twice a week after I came back to Chicago."

"You mean after you walked away from me at Heathrow."

"Yes, when I walked away from . . ." Margo let her voice trail off. "It was painful going back to the cafe."

"Why did you?" Freddy pushed. "I'm curious."

"Please, Freddy," Margo rubbed her elbow. "Where are we going with this?"

"Why, Margo? Why did you go there?"

Her answer took a while coming. "Because I dreamed that maybe I'd see you walk in and head for my table. I wanted that more than anything. But you never . . ."

Sensing Margo's discomfort, Freddy viewed the paintings on the walls, as if in a museum. Margo sank in the couch and watched him. There were family photographs, too, and on the mantle over the fireplace a photograph of the old gang standing with arms around one another, their smiles wide, faces filled with hope.

"We were so young," Freddy said.

"Remember where it was taken?" Margo continued watching him.

The photograph was taken in front of the little fountain outside the conservatory on the night of Kreutzer Trio's premiere concert. All three were in their senior year at the conservatory. Howard, in his senior year at Northwestern with a business major, did all the publicity for them.

Freddy brushed a hand on the photo and laughed. "You remember it was also the night old Howie experienced Mindy, The Crusher."

Margo laughed. "I forgot about her. Oh my God. Mindy. What a bruiser. All the girls were afraid of her. She played the oboe, didn't she?"

"Baritone sax. Fitting instrument for Mindy. Big mama." Freddy kept laughing. "Wasn't all that Mindy played, though."

"I could have killed you for throwing poor Howard to her like meat to a caged tiger." Margo was laughing. "Oh my God. Poor Howard. So sweet and innocent."

Freddy was bent over now and holding his stomach. "Old Howie disappeared the entire weekend, gone, and I mean we had no idea where the hell he was."

"And then for the rest of the week, whenever I saw him, he kept grinning and babbling to himself," Margo said, her voice shaking from the laughter. "You were such a devil, Freddy." She suddenly wiped off her laugh. "You didn't . . . with Mindy?"

"No, sugar, I only had eyes for you." Freddy slipped behind the piano. "Like the song." He played a few bars from "I Only Have Eyes for You" and then segued into the 18th Variation from Rachmaninoff's Rhapsody on a Theme of Paganini. Half way through the music he stopped, his mood changed. "What happened to us, Margo?" he said.

Margo moved to the window and stood watching the rain. "Life happened, Freddy. Not every story has a happy ending. Ours didn't."

"But why us? I mean if we didn't love each other, that's one thing. We did love each other, didn't we?"

"Did we love each other?" she sighed. "I loved you so much it hurt. Damn you, Freddy."

"I deserve that."

"Yes, you deserve it, damn you." Margo rubbed her elbow. "And I deserve it, because I didn't even try to find a middle ground." Then she broke into tears.

"Oh Margo." Freddy shuffled to the window. "You're tearing me up. Please don't."

He wrapped her in his arms. Her body felt warm, sensuous. It felt familiar, even after all the years. She buried her face in the small of his neck, shuddering in his arms. How strange a feeling, Freddy thought, how weird a sensation. It was Heathrow all over again, except that this time they were not saying goodbye, but lamenting having said it.

Margo then broke away from him and ran upstairs. It was a while before she came back into the living room with a tray of tea and pastries. She had freshened up, but her eyes were pink from crying.

Freddy, playing a Chopin nocturn, stopped and followed her with his eyes as she placed the tray on the coffee table. "Feeling better, sugar?" He closed the piano lid and came over to the couch.

Margo handed him a cup of tea. "I don't suppose you've seen last night's review."

"Never read reviews, you know that."

"Well, for your information, the man raved about your performance."

"You know what the great Eric Satie said?"

"Why do I feel one of your stories coming?"

Freddy smiled and sipped his tea. "Sugar, you still know how to make good tea, *like them English folk*."

"For heaven's sake, Freddy, what did Satie say?"

"Satie said he worked up several lectures on intelligence and musicality in animals. Today he was going to speak about intelligence and musicality in critics. Same subject."

Margo regarded Freddy, and then smiled.

"I love your smile, sugar," Freddy said. His mobile phone rang and he answered. Phil was on the line asking to meet him for breakfast the next morning at his hotel to get more details for the profile he was writing on him. Freddy okayed the time.

"You look tired," Margo said.

"It's been a grinding season." Freddy thought a moment. "I've done too much in my life, Margo. Pushed too hard."

"Sounds like a confession."

"Maybe it is."

"Because the Freddy I knew played seven days a week and twice on Sunday," Margo reminded him.

"Yeah, I know that Freddy."

"My God, I've never known anyone with such musical passion. Such intensity. Like a narcotic."

"I ate and slept the piano before I could put my britches on."

"Do you still?"

"What, put on my britches?"

"I hope so."

Freddy chuckled, running a hand through his hair. It was still damp. "A long time ago Luke told me not to live inside the Steinway."

"And you went right ahead and did it anyway."

"It was the only way for me and you never understood that."

"No, Freddy, I understood perfectly well," Margo argued. "You just forgot the difference between a commitment and a Mozart score."

"Marriage, you mean."

"Of course, I mean marriage," Margo snapped. "God, you make me crazy. What was wrong with that if two people were in love the way we were? That's how it's done, Freddy."

"Like Robert and Clara Schumann," he said.

"You're not funny."

"I wasn't trying to be."

"Oh, shut up. I'm tired of this." Margo poured another cup of tea for herself and ignored Freddy. "Other musicians were married and managed a home and family, but not the great Frederick Priestley."

"We soared in art and stumbled everywhere else."

"Only you stumbled everywhere else. You! You! You!"

"And that's been my torment all these years." Freddy reached for his cup, but it was empty. "One of my many torments, anyway."

"What's the use?" Margo said. "Gone and forgotten." She suddenly marched off and slipped in a CD of Schubert's Trout Quintet in the player and stood listening at the window.

"I love the Trout," Freddy said.

"Rain and more rain." Margo sighed, ignoring his comment. "Where do you go next? I mean after the anniversary."

"Back to London," he said.

"Long enough to change socks?"

"Long rest is more like it. I'm tired."

"You sure you know how to rest?"

Freddy ignored the dig. "Home cooked food, tea in the garden with Marguerite. Full throttle domestic."

"The Freddy I knew was as domestic as Marco Polo," Margo said.

"Well, your wife and Marguerite will like having you home, I'm sure."

"Marguerite will," Freddy said with resolve, "but Gabrielle and I live in different worlds."

The comment surprised Margo. "I had heard rumors, but . . ."

"All true, probably."

"I'm sorry. I had no idea it was that bad between you. I mean I've seen photos and you look like a pair of love birds."

Freddy blew out a breath and shrugged. "We try to keep a front with Marguerite, and the press, but I think our marriage has crashed and burned."

"I'm sorry for you, Freddy."

"I saw what my parents had and then look at me," he lamented.

Margo returned to the couch and handed the CD cover to Freddy. "You look so handsome. And Marguerite is an angel." She paused and thought. "Gabrielle is gorgeous. No wonder you . . ." Her voice trailed off.

The photo was taken four years earlier and it pictured Freddy with Marguerite on his shoulders and his arm around Gabrielle. All three glowed in the Austrian sunshine.

"Was a great time," Freddy said, touching his temple, "and no gray hair then."

Freddy made the recording in a little church in Steyer, not far from Vienna, where in 1819 Schubert began writing the quintet. "One of the happiest times in Schubert's short life," Freddy explained to Gabrielle over dinner back then. "Trout is light hearted and sunny overall, and you can't help humming the set of variations in the fourth movement on Schubert's song 'Die Forelle' ('The Trout')."

Gabrielle was between films and Freddy convinced her to make the journey as a family vacation of sorts: a two-week escape in Schubert's sunshine. He loved Gabrielle then and thought she loved him. And they had Marguerite. The recording took about a week: the quintet along with a Schubert piano trio and a pair of impromptus on the same CD.

Freddy rehearsed and recorded in the morning and the rest of the day he spent with Gabrielle and Marguerite. They wandered around the city and the surrounding areas, ate ice cream, read in cafes, and watched Marguerite play in the park. Freddy was happy: his career flourished, had a stunning wife and a little girl who took his breath away.

"My time in Steyer gives me an inkling of what my parents must have had together," Freddy wrote to Rufus. "If I had only half of what they had."

"Those cats had their own little number," Rufus wrote back. "Time you stopped thinking about that. Find your own place in the universe."

Freddy took a bite of the croissant in his plate and leaned back. "Schubert said he came into the world for no other purpose but to compose. How I feel about the piano, Margo. We're like twins. But I'm surprised you have the Trout recording."

"Why wouldn't I have it?" Margo frowned. "I have all of your recordings — the Beethoven piano concerto set, the Brahms . . ." She paused. "Stop looking at me like that."

Freddy realized he was listening to her and imagining the warmth of her breath against his lips. "Looking like what?"

"Like you're doing now. Please don't, Freddy."

"Sorry, sugar. Was I that obvious?"

"Yes, you were, and it's not right," Margo said.

No, it was not, Freddy reminded himself. He thought he was okay as long as he was far away from Margo. Sitting across from her now, though, he was far from okay.

"Well," he said finally, "let's get out of here before this thing turns into a wake." His coat was dry now and he put it on. "But before we go," he said, "answer me this. Did you love Howard?"

"Yes, I did," Margo shot back. "Why do you even ask?" Then she thought a moment. "But not the way I loved you. Is that what you want to hear, Freddy?"

15

Rufus used to joke that he'd played the tenor sax at the Jazz Notebook since jazz was invented. He came up from New Orleans with Effie for a short gig at the southside Chicago jazz club and ended up staying. Occasionally Effie sang with Rufus's quartet. Later Rufus led the conservatory's jazz studies program, as well.

In the old days Rufus invited Freddy for the Friday night jam sessions and gave his star student room to stretch. Freddy blew away the crowd, according to Rufus. Margo said she couldn't believe what a sensation Freddy was, and Rufus said he heard Freddy every day at the conservatory and still couldn't believe his ears.

That evening, when Freddy came into the club with Margo as promised earlier in the week, Rufus had just finished a set with his quartet. "Missy, darlin', you do an old man's heart's good." He hugged Margo.

"Margo's been on Michigan Avenue too long, Ruf," Freddy said, pulling the chair out for her.

"Ah, Missy darlin', this is where the real people are," Rufus said, and sat down.

"You two, I swear . . ." Margo took Rufus's hands. "How are you, my darling?"

"Fine now that I've got my kids with me," Rufus said. Rufus and Effie had no children and Rufus always referred to his students as his kids.

"I'm afraid this kid wasn't exactly the cream of your jazz crop, not like wonder boy here." Margo flipped her head at Freddy.

"Wonder boy was always inspired when you were around, Margo," Freddy said.

"It's what I told my Effie," Rufus said. "Little Missy here is the most beautiful girl in Chicago."

By then it was time to play again. Rufus introduced Freddy on the little stage as the great concert pianist home at the club to play America's true art form. And home Freddy was, and once again Rufus gave him room to stretch. The crowd loved it. Rufus beamed at his former star student. Years earlier, Margo asked Freddy if he felt like two different people playing classical music and jazz.

"Same person," Freddy answered. "I Sit at the keyboard and it flows out of me. Billy Strayhorn or the great Ludwig, I don't open and close musical doors. They're always open and I go in, whichever I fancy at the time."

Before leaving the club to drive Margo home, Freddy promised Rufus to bring her over for Effie's chili.

On the way home in the car, Margo wiped a small tear. "I'd forgotten how much I loved that old man."

"Rufus gave us everything he had," Freddy said, "and he gave me the world."

"Should have at least called Rufus," Margo said, "but I was such a mess and wanted to forget everything. Just curl up and close my eyes."

"I'm sorry, sugar."

Margo did not respond. She lowered the window and put her head back on the seat. The air was cool and damp. "That's why I never wrote to you," she continued. "I mean wrote, long letters, but then tore them up."

"Seems we both did, but mine stayed in my head." Freddy stopped at a traffic light and lit a cigar. "I was going to make it as a concert pianist no matter what, Margo. Can you understand that?"

She nodded yes. "Little Margo was an obstacle in your way."

"You were the love of my life," Freddy said, hiding behind his cigar smoke for a moment, "but I still sacrificed you and the wound still bleeds inside me."

Margo sat up and took a deep breath.

"I love you, Margo," Freddy said. "Nothing will ever change that."

She touched his arm. "Please don't say anymore."

No, of course not, Freddy told himself. Except that after they parted in London, he himself was a mess. Catastrophic mess. The streets of London witnessed his plight. He walked them day and night. Weeks. Months. He felt like an amnesiac completely lost.

Soon his money was gone. Rufus wrote, "Pull yourself together, boy. You made your choice. Do anything you have to. Survive any way you can. You're a pianist. That's your art. Use it to make your way through this mess."

Freddy's agent Bob Chase found him a steady gig as hotel cocktail pianist until he could line up some concerts for him. Freddy liked the job: the music was sweet and the tips good. He met Gabrielle there, although nothing was to become of it until years later, when he ran into her in Paris. By then, he was a world-renowned concert pianist.

Freddy left his thoughts and asked Margo if she was warm enough. She nodded yes and kept looking out the window. They rode in silence the rest of the way. When he walked her to the door, Margo went inside without saying anything and closed the door. Freddy stood there puzzled by her behavior, wondering if he offended her, but then he was too tired to make a big case out of it.

Back in his hotel room Freddy checked the rest of his messages. Gabrielle had called: "Cheri, call me at the Paris apartment. We need to talk."

Talk about what? Didn't they say everything that needed to be said? Freddy wasn't in the mood for Gabrielle and decided to call her later. When he called Marguerite, she was excited about her violin performance in class. "Oh honey, I sent them whistling to Cairo," she said. Freddy laughed. Connie's favorite saying in the Mae West imitation rendered by a nine-year-old with a thick British accent was priceless. Whenever Freddy asked his mother how their show went, Connie always hugged him and murmured, "Oh honey, we sent them whistling to Cairo."

Freddy took his memories to the window and stood looking out. It was a while before he forced himself to check his other messages.

Bob Chase booked several more engagements for the upcoming season: Berlin, Barcelona and Birmingham. Bob also wanted to know if Freddy was up for complete recordings of Debussy and Ravel. "We'd talked about that, you remember?" he said. "Also, let's think about the complete Iberia by Albeniz, one of your favorites."

Freddy called Bob and left a message giving him the go-ahead on everything. "Also, Bob," he added, "I want to record a tribute to Luke and Connie. Do some of the great songs they did, like 'Skylark,' 'Moonray,' 'Lush Life,' you know, a collection of the sweet stuff. Mom loved them." He poured himself a drink. "I've thought about the recording for years. We'll have to find a singer with Mom's special cabaret sound. No idea who. I'll be on piano. Got to do it as a tribute to a remarkable musical couple — Luke and Connie, my parents."

Freddy telephoned Gabrielle after all, but got the answering machine. He left no message. There was another message from Phil reminding him about the breakfast interview. There were several requests for media interviews. He decided to deal with them later. Sheila Brentwood called to remind him of the dinner at George Paulik's house in Lake Forest on Sunday. Sheila also invited him for a small gathering of friends at her downtown condo after his recital Saturday night. "And bring Phil," she added.

Well now, Freddy thought, his old friend Phil and Sheila Brentwood: it could work. Obviously, there was chemistry between them. He took his drink back to the window and stood watching the little lights twinkling in the distance over the black waters of Lake Michigan.

16

"We say I do and before we know it, we're not doing," Phil told Freddy over breakfast in the hotel dining room. "Look, half of my married friends in New York are running on empty."

"So what went wrong with the marriage?" Freddy poured them coffee from the thermos left on the table. "I mean it didn't happen overnight."

"I don't know exactly what went wrong," Phil said. "Reached a point where we didn't click anymore. One day you're happy together and in love and then it all goes sour. We just didn't make each other happy anymore."

His own story with Gabrielle, Freddy believed. Not that he didn't see it coming: Separate bedrooms, no love making, laughter gone, arguments. They were just unhappy together.

"Did you even click with her from the start, just like that, I mean?" Freddy snapped his fingers.

"Nothing as romantic as that. It took its time picking up steam."

"With Gabrielle," Freddy said, "passion masked everything else. I realized that in time. Then Marguerite came along and that changed my life." He sipped his coffee and thought. "I loved Gabrielle, but probably not enough, not the way I felt about Margo. Then again, Margo is a once in a lifetime experience."

Freddy met Gabrielle at a vulnerable stage in their lives: She grew up in a home plagued by tragedy and was always desperate for love.

Freddy gave her what she needed, at least for a while. Freddy himself, despite a flourishing career as a concert pianist, and a healthy love life, never stopped searching for what Luke and Connie had. Yet he was the first to admit, and Rufus told him many times, that what his parents had was as elusive for anyone else as the fountain of youth. That included their boy.

Phil took out a mini recorder from his briefcase. "In the end it was no use going on and making each other more unhappy," he said.

"Do you still love her?"

"I don't know," Phil said. "She's a wonderful woman. Very attractive. And a loving mother to our twins. We had some good times. But do I still love her? Did I ever?" Phil tinkered with the mini recorder. "We weren't Freddy and Margo."

"Our little Margo, oh yes." Freddy finished his coffee. "Having her around now is no damn help with all my Gabrielle issues."

"You've got a mess on your hands, old buddy," Phil said, pulling out his reporter's notebook from the briefcase. "Wouldn't want to be in your shoes." He switched on the recorder. "Now, I'm going to make you sound like the ivory tickler with a halo."

"Thanks," Freddy snickered, "but I know a pair of scorned women who'd take a stick to the halo."

Later in his room, Freddy telephoned Gabrielle in Paris, but there was no answer. He left her a message to call him. No answer on her mobile either. He left the same message there. Before meeting Phil, he left Gabrielle another message to call him.

Marguerite and Nanny were preparing for dinner, when Freddy called. Marguerite wanted to know more about their upcoming cross-country trip in America. The Rocky Mountains in Colorado, the Wasatch in Utah, Freddy told her. "And we'll go on lots of trails and do some rafting," he added. "And we'll visit a few ghost towns. Me and my little sugar exploring America."

Marguerite asked about his recital. "Beethoven, Schubert, and opening with Chopin's Ballad No. 1," he said. "What do you think of a Spanish dance by Manuel de Falla for encore?"

"Oh Daddy, that is splendid," Marguerite said."

"I hope the audience fancies the concert."

"They will adore you, Daddy."

"Adore the way I adore you?"

"But of course, my good man," Marguerite put on her royal robe, chuckling.

Oh, how he loved that little girl.

17

In the months before Freddy came to Chicago for the conservatory's anniversary celebration, the walls began closing in on him. He grew restless and often escaped to the streets, whether in London or abroad for concerts. He walked for hours. He faded away in cafes.

Sometimes he took Marguerite with him when playing abroad, if she was off from school, and she went to his rehearsal and then to the concert. They wandered around cities, dined in fine restaurants. They visited some of Europe's greatest capitols. Before Marguerite was born, Gabrielle traveled with Freddy when not filming. He loved having her with him, although Gabrielle didn't have his wandering spirit, or Marguerite's.

Freddy wrote Effie and Rufus that Marguerite shared his passion for wandering around cities. Effie thought they both got the itch from Luke. "Oh honey," Effie wrote, "that man could walk the streets from morning till night like he was measuring them. And when your Mama went with him, he was in heaven."

Putting aside the memories, Freddy called Sheila and accepted the invitation to her little party that evening. He declined her offer to send a limousine for him, opting instead to walk after a change of clothing following his recital.

With the walls closing in on him again, Freddy fled his hotel room for Margo's shop. The bright sunshine painting Michigan Avenue lifted his spirit. It also brought back memory of another walk on Michigan Avenue long ago.

It was the day after one of Kreutzer Trio's concerts and he and Margo were clipping along to meet Phil for lunch at a little bistro on Rush Street when out of the blue Margo suddenly announced, "Freddy, when I walk, do my boobs bounce?"

Margo's unlikely question, coming from someone with her proper upbringing, caught Freddy off guard. "Your what?"

"Do my boobs bounce when I walk?" Margo repeated.

Freddy, still unsure of what he heard, gave Margo a puzzled look.

"For heaven's sake, Freddy, do my boobs bounce when I walk?" She rolled her eyes. "Sheeesh . . ."

Freddy craned his neck. "Sugar, your sweet boobs bounce in an intoxicating combination of the Austrian landler and the Brazilian samba."

"Oh good." Margo blew out a breath.

"Anything about your boobs is of interest to me," Freddy said, still puzzled, "but why do you ask?"

"Well, I noticed a couple gorgeous women giving you the eye and their boobs bounced." Margo shrugged all too innocently. "So I wondered, you know, if mine didn't, I'd have to do something about it."

"And what do you have in mind?"

"Oh, I don't know. Have you teach them the landler and the samba, maybe."

"Glad to help out, sugar," Freddy chuckled.

Recalling the incident to Margo at the shop, they both burst out laughing. Freddy loved her laughter. He loved everything about her, bouncing boobs and all. He looked around the boutique, still trying to envision Margo as a shop keeper. "Very tasteful," he said, "but you always did have good taste."

Margo nodded. "Sometimes it does feel a little weird."

"Especially since you were a hell of fiddler."

"For your information, buddy, I still am." Margo took Freddy's hand and gave him a tour of the shop. "I'm hungry. You?" she said.

Freddy checked his watch. It was noon. "Late breakfast with Phil, but I'll take you to lunch."

In the café, Margo apologized for her behavior the night before. "I forgot my manners, and I know how much you hate bad manners."

"Well, I'm sure you had your reasons."

"No excuse for the way I acted. It's just that you do something to me."

"Ah, Cole Porter." Freddy tried to lighten up the mood and began singing the tune in a low voice.

Margo listened. "You never cease to surprise me, Freddy," she said. "I didn't know you sang. All these years and no idea."

"I learned fast as a cocktail pianist and singer in London . . . after you . . ."

Margo paused a moment and then finished his thought: "After I left you."

The waiter brought Margo a sandwich and Freddy a beer. Margo studied her plate. Freddy then watched her bite into her sandwich. He slid his beer over to her.

Margo took a sip of the beer and then leaned back in the booth. "Hmmmm."

"What?"

"Another time, Freddy, at a wild party long ago, you let me have a sip of your drink, remember?"

He remembered: "I'm my jolly old self with a Jack Daniels and a Cohiba and I see this beautiful creature. She leaves me breathless. I'm instantly in love."

"And here's this beautiful boy leaning against the kitchen counter like the king of something or other, so sure of himself, so audacious," Margo followed. "He has this shimmering golden mane, shoulder length, and he looks like a young Franz Liszt in those old photographs." Margo took another bite of her sandwich. "I catch myself walking toward him and there's music in his heart. My God, I can hear it. Little insanity in his head. I can feel it. I know nothing about him, but I'm already in love with him."

Margo picked up her sandwich and put it down. Her eyes filled with tears.

"Margo," Freddy reached for her hand and she withdrew it.

"Oh God, why did you have to come back, Freddy? Why didn't you stay away?" Margo began sobbing hard, her face covered in her hands. "What do you want from me?"

"Don't know what to say, sugar."

"I want answers," she whimpered. "I need to know."

A mobile phone rang nearby and a man with a booming voice answered. Freddy made a sour face and shook his head in frustration. What was that about manners?

"I want Perfection," Freddy said. "What Luke and Connie had. What we had for a while."

"We had it, Freddy, but you gave it up for your piano." Margo studied him, as if reading his mind. "If you were trying to make us into your parents, it was wrong to do. We had different needs. Yours was music."

"Sounds like you hold it against me."

Margo's tone softened. She wiped her tears. "No, no, Freddy, my beautiful Freddy, I hold nothing against you. We had different needs . . . at the time."

"I did make a bloody mess of things, didn't I?"

"I had my share in that, Freddy, but it's done. The past. Let it go."

A young couple came in, arms around each other, and waited to be seated. The man whispered something to the girl and then kissed her ear.

"Letting go isn't easy for me, Margo," Freddy said. "I can't wash it out of me. It's there. It haunts me."

18

ichigan Avenue was their *Avenue des Champs-Elysee*, Freddy told Margo long ago, and promised that someday they would stroll down the real one, what Parisians call the most beautiful avenue in the world — *La plus belle avenue du monde*. He did keep his promise when Kreutzer Trio played in Paris.

On the way back to *Swan* after lunch, Freddy reminded Margo of their many strolls down the Champs-Elysees.

"*La plus belle avenue du monde*," Margo said, and took his arm. "How well I remember."

Having Margo so close to him felt a little strange, even awkward, but the feeling lasted a blink. Margo was as warm and soft, assuring, as Freddy remembered. In the early days in Chicago, Freddy often talked about Kreutzer Trio playing the big time all over the world. Margo usually just nodded and said nothing. Her attitude frustrated him. Finally he questioned her lukewarm enthusiasm for his elaborate plans.

"My parents are here and my friends," Margo said. "All of my memories are here. I met the love of my life here, Freddy — you. Chicago's my home."

"We'll have the world for our home, sugar," Freddy kept on. "We can make a home anywhere we want."

"I'm not sure, Freddy," Margo confessed. "I don't have gypsy blood me. A real home is what I want. A stable home, with children, and the grandparents nearby to spoil them. "

It was on such a stroll on Michigan Avenue a few days after they met that Freddy posed the trio idea to Margo. Phil, who played a mean cello, according to Freddy, was already onboard. "Piano, violin and cello," Freddy said. "Kreutzer Trio."

"I see you've figured out everything." Margo gave him a little smile.

Before long, with Howard as their agent, until his family shipped him off to Northwestern, the trio was playing private parties and weddings around town. Freddy dug up a pile of salon music and arranged it for piano trio: Kalman, Stolz, Lehar, Kreisler, Levitzky and a playlist of other composers oozing with European charm. All the while, he also kept up a solo career, giving recitals and performing with community orchestras.

Later, the private parties and salon music behind them, Freddy convinced Margo and Phil to make London home base for the trio. Margo didn't want to leave Chicago, and her parents wondered why London. Freddy assured them that London was the center of the universe.

Bob Chase, their agent, booked the trio around European cities. Small venues initially. The trio had ways to go to be in the same class as other great trios, past and present, but Freddy promised Margo and Phil that at least they were good enough to be noticed.

All that ended for the trio until the conservatory celebration, when the three planned to get together for one performance.

Freddy closed his memories and pulled Margo closer. At a stoplight, she rested her head against his shoulder. "Notice how the older we get the less sure we are of things?" she murmured.

"Growing up isn't what it's hyped up to be," Freddy proclaimed. "It's a pain in the ass." He kissed Margo's forehead. Her skin felt soft, enticing, and he loved her fragrance. He loved her gravity.

They stopped at a men's clothing store, where Freddy saw a suit in the display window he liked, and Margo said he would look handsome in it. He tried the suit on, chose a tie, shoes, and a fedora, too, and had the store send them to his hotel.

Outside *Swan* Margo confessed, "I don't want to be the cause of your marriage breaking up. It's not right."

"My marriage broke up in spirit a while ago."

"Then fix it," Margo snapped.

"I've tried, but we're like guests in our home, Gabrielle and I. We don't do anything together anymore. I wouldn't be surprised if we introduce ourselves every morning and exchanged business cards."

"This is so sad, Freddy." Margo wiped a tear.

Gabrielle came from a family in war with itself and she carried the scars, Freddy told Margo. He said he tried to live with those scars, hoping that in time she would overcome her demons. When Marguerite came along, Gabrielle did so for a time, but she began sinking back into the abyss and he could not pull her out, Freddy explained.

"Sometimes I see us locked inside a speeding car without breaks," he confessed to Margo.

"Don't talk like that." She shuddered. "You're scaring me."

"I have nightmares about it myself."

"Oh God, I don't want to hear this talk. Please, Freddy, I don't want anything happening to you."

Freddy checked his watch. He planned to spend some practice time at the piano in the concert hall before heading back to his hotel for a nap. A light dinner, then, and on to the concert hall for the recital.

"Nothing will happen to me, sugar," he promised, and kissed Margo's brow.

Margo turned around in the entrance to her shop. "You still like meatloaf? Effie's recipe."

"That and a cold beer and I'm your slave, sugar."

"Well, we don't have to go that far," Margo said with a frown. "Come to the house after the recital — the kids are spending the night at Mom and Dad's."

"How can I refuse such an enticing offer?"

"Nothing is happening except for the meatloaf, in case you're reading something into it. I'm not that slick."

"Not reading anything, sugar. Meatloaf rules."

Freddy also told Margo about Sheila's party and that he would come for the grub after that. Margo smiled and kissed him on the cheek. He turned to leave and stopped. "By the way, sugar, when you walk, your boobs still bounce. Sweet to look at."

"Oh good," Margo announced.

Later in his hotel room, Freddy telephoned Gabrielle's mobile. She answered, groggy. "Oh it's you, the husband," she muttered. There was music and noise.

"Are you all right?"

"Fine and dandy." Her speech slurred. She coughed.

"We're having another blast, are we?" He shouldn't even ask. "How much have you had to drink?"

"I'm a free woman and do as I please."

"And you have a husband and a daughter." Freddy was trying hard to keep calm. "Where are you, in Paris?"

"My favorite place in the world."

Ice surged through Freddy's spine. "Destroying yourself isn't the solution, Gabrielle. Think about your family. Okay, if not me, think about Marguerite. Think about you."

Freddy squeezed his temples. A headache before a performance he didn't need. Gabrielle was drunk, and he was sure stoned on something, too. With Marguerite around, Gabrielle was the perfect mother at home in London. Paris, on the other hand, was her wilderness. "Gabrielle, I beg of you, don't do this," Freddy said. "Send those bums home, whoever you have there, and go to bed before something bad happens."

"And you go to bed with your girlfriend." Gabrielle laughed. Then she cried. "Who makes better love to you, Gabrielle or your girlfriend?"

There was no use. At this stage, talking to her was like dancing with a robot. "Frankly, Gabrielle, it's been so long with the both of you that I can't remember," he said.

"I hate you, Freddy," Gabrielle shouted.

"Hate me all you want, but don't hate Gabrielle." He was running out of words, and out of patience. "Listen," he tried one more time, "after I finish up in Chicago, we can talk. Go somewhere quiet and relax. Majorca, maybe. Anywhere you want. Be sensible, please." But he was talking to a silent phone.

He thought of cancelling his appearances and flying to Paris, but that would do as much good as it did twice before. Forget the embarrassment it caused him after cancelling his concerts almost at the last minute. "What do you want me to do?" he begged Bob Chase. "She's my wife and I have to keep her from blowing herself up."

With Gabrielle draining every bit of energy out of him, this time around Freddy questioned if he had it in him to send them whistling to Cairo. Then he heard Luke's voice: "The Priestley boys, father and son, go out there and play even if the world is ending. It's the only way for us, my little man."

19

Sheila Brentwood lived in a luxurious condo in a downtown high-rise overlooking Lake Michigan. Inside, the black and white glitz matched the glass and steel of the towers outside. Chairs and couches in white blended into the plush white carpeting. A large glass-topped dining room table would probably accommodate an army of guests, Freddy thought. A collection of modern art completed the dazzling picture. The only thing missing was a concert grand in the shape of a rocket ship, he told himself. At least there was a massive sound system.

Sheila obliged the astonished Freddy and announced, "From a different period in my life that now I regret."

"Dazzling," Freddy said, craving the wood and leather in his house.

Sheila looked radiant in black silk pants and white sequin top. She wore a brilliant diamond necklace. A beautiful woman, yes, but Freddy wasn't sure how Phil fit in her lifestyle. Phil had not taken his eyes off of Sheila at the post-concert gathering in Freddy's big dressing room. Or would Sheila be comfortable with Phil's austere tastes? Then again, Freddy thought of Effie's dictum: that if it was meant to be . . .

Sheila curtsied when she noticed Freddy's eyes on her. "Margo's selections," she said.

"Margo has good taste, and a beautiful subject to work with."

"Thank you, sir." Sheila kissed Freddy on the cheek. She

introduced him to the other guests, who were full of praise for his performance. Then she said, "All this praise must be boring by now."

"It's only boring when the compliments stop coming," Freddy assured her. "Then you wonder if you're washed up as a pianist or the audience is moving on."

"Would that be the worst thing in your life?"

It was an odd question coming from Sheila, Freddy thought. "Losing my daughter is — the worst thing that can happen to me." The thought sent a chill through him. "And losing my hands is right up there."

"And your wife?"

Freddy hesitated, thinking Sheila must have heard the rumors about his shaky marriage. "Gabrielle, too, yes, of course," he said, not sure if he meant it.

Sheila flashed a naughty smile. "Ah, Mister Priestley, that sounded like an afterthought."

A wee bit too bold are we now, sister? Freddy told himself.

The maid brought a tray of drinks for them. "Jack Daniels and a quarter note of water," Sheila said proudly. "If I'm not mistaken, that's what some gentlemen from the south prefer." A champagne for her.

Freddy nodded his thanks. Again, he took note of how stunning Sheila looked. No wonder Phil was losing his sanity over her.

"Margo's been a lot of help," Sheila said.

"Help in what?"

"Your preferences, likes and dislikes. I wanted to welcome you properly." Sheila lifted her champagne and toasted, "To homecomings."

New guests arrived and Sheila excused herself. Freddy found his way to the balcony, where high-rise lights glittered around him, and far off over Lake Michigan, tiny boat lights twinkled in the black water. It was an overwhelming site, and a reflection of his life, Freddy thought. Powerful forces pulled him in different directions. He was taking a beating. He was worn out. He was whipped. Gabrielle took it all out of him. Margo did so by just being there. Again, he questioned his decision to come to Chicago. If Margo was a recurring dream until then, now she was the morning light that blinded him.

"I see you've discovered my favorite hiding place," Freddy heard Sheila say. She sidled against the railing and regarded him. She also had a fresh drink for him.

"Makes you feel like you're flying in a dream." Freddy toasted her.

"It's the perfect elevation for reflecting on life," Sheila said, "and for hiding from some of life's realities."

Freddy studied her. No wonder every man and his cousin crumbled before her striking looks, he thought. "What makes you think I'm hiding?"

"Just a feeling, I guess," Sheila said. "Don't we sometimes hide to escape?"

"Is that what I'm doing?"

"Or else I'm scaring you."

"All women scare me." Freddy took a big swig from his drink. It was perfectly done.

"Funny, but that's my line about men."

"Beautiful woman like you? Dripping with wealth. Men lining up outside your door."

"Yes, but not the right men, I'm afraid. Twice burned and that's enough."

"Their loss."

"That's what I keep telling myself."

Phil was the only suitor to ignore Sheila's fortune and social standing, Freddy was sure, knowing his old friend. "You might still find that gem," he said.

"If I were treasure hunting." Sheila breathed in the night and closed her eyes. "I'm finding being alone isn't necessarily like being lonely."

"But never hurts to leave the door open."

"I suppose not," Sheila agreed.

Freddy checked his watch. It was nearly midnight and Margo expected him.

"Yes, you must be exhausted," Sheila said.

"And I have rehearsals tomorrow."

At the door, Sheila gave Freddy a kiss on the cheek. "Until dinner tomorrow evening at George Paulik's, Mister Priestley."

"Friends call me Freddy. After all, you gave me drinks and let me share your balcony." Freddy thought a moment. "By the way, Phil fancies you a lot."

"Thanks for telling me," Sheila said. "I think I like him quite a bit myself."

20

Freddy took a taxi from Sheila's to the hotel and then drove to Margo's. On the way, he called Gabrielle at the Paris apartment and had to leave a message. No go with her mobile either. Who knew where she was, or what she was doing, and with whom? When Gabrielle went on a binge, Freddy never knew what to expect.

Sometimes Gabrielle chose not to answer his calls, and sometimes Freddy was grateful, knowing that conversation often led to conflict. This night, however, he was frightened for her. Maybe it was because of the blowout with her earlier in the day. Most of all, he was afraid for Marguerite should Gabrielle drive herself over the edge.

Freddy was still struggling with his nightmare when Margo opened the door in her robe, sleep in her eyes. "I was beginning to wonder if Sheila tucked you in," she said, and led him into the kitchen.

"What gave you that idea?" Freddy thought Margo looked lovely.

"Well, it did cross my mind only for a moment."

"That I would look at someone else? Shucks, Margo, I'm disappointed."

"But I also left a candle in the window thinking you had enough sense."

"How well you know me."

"I thought I did once upon a time."

"Go ahead, Margo, drive the knife deeper. Dig it in all the way. I deserve it."

"I don't carry a knife, Freddy, you know that."

Margo offered him a chair at the kitchen table and then put a plate of cold meatloaf with sliced tomatoes and cucumber in front of him. A bottle of cold beer and a frosted mug, too.

"I'd travel the world for Effie's meatloaf."

"If you please, buddy, Effie's recipe and little Margo's interpretation."

"Delicious, just like the chef."

"You should know."

"Oh sugar, how well I know," Freddy said, beaming.

Margo studied him. "You look tired."

"Worn out like an old piano." Freddy washed the meatloaf down with the beer.

Still regarding him, Margo added, "And you look sad. What's wrong?

"It doesn't matter."

"Of course, it matters, Freddy," she snapped. "We share too many years. It matters to me."

Freddy took his beer to the kitchen window. The outside lights threw a peaceful filter over Margo's backyard. He remembered all the nights he perched in the window seat in the little house in New Orleans waiting for Luke and Connie to come home from a gig. Sometimes he fell asleep and woke up to Luke carrying him upstairs and saying, "Famous concert pianists need their rest, my little man."

"Oh Daddy, I miss you so much," Freddy remembered saying on those nights. "Sometimes I'm scared you and Mom won't come home."

Margo shook his thoughts. "What's wrong, Freddy? For God's sake, tell me."

Everything was wrong. His life teetered on the edge of a cliff with his past and present fighting to see which pushed him over the edge first. Gabrielle took it out of him. Seeing Margo out of his reach tortured him.

"Freddy, please."

He returned to the table and told her everything.

When he finished, Margo watched him fiddle with the beer bottle. "My God, what have you done to yourself, Freddy?" she uttered. "It breaks my heart to see what's happened to you. This isn't my Freddy. I don't know who you are."

Freddy asked the same questions of himself a million times. "Sometimes I think I'm being punished for what I did to you and Gabrielle's my punishment."

"There must've been a time when you were happy."

"Yes, sure," Freddy said. "I thought I was doing a hell of a job getting over you, and Gabrielle seemed happy. We needed each other, each for a different reason, and we held on for dear life just to survive." Freddy drank the rest of his beer. "Look, I knew nothing about Gabrielle's life except for what I read in the newspapers and saw on TV. We both came with heavy baggage, that much we knew about each other."

Margo brought him another beer.

Freddy took a long drink and sank in the chair. He thought back to the first time he saw Gabrielle. He was playing in that hotel lounge in London and trying to put his life together. Gabrielle leaned on the grand piano and requested music from the film Sabrina, which starred Humphrey Bogart and Audrey Hepburn.

Freddy played "Isn't it Romantic" and "My Silent Love," both standards that were incorporated into the film score. Gabrielle thanked him with a kiss on the cheek. Six years later Freddy was wandering in Montmartre when Gabrielle tapped him on the shoulder. "You've come a long way from Sabrina," she announced.

Earlier in the evening she heard Freddy perform Chopin's first piano concerto with the Paris Orchestra. She was impressed, she told him. Gabrielle was 26 and just out of a troubled affair with an Italian actor.

"Long way from Sabrina, yes," Freddy said, "but if I knew I'd see you again, I would have driven faster."

Margo reached over and took Freddy's hand. "Penny for your thoughts."

Freddy squeezed her hands. They were as warm and loving as he remembered. "I looked for Margo in all the women I met and she wasn't there."

Margo's eyes welled up in tears.

"There was no sign of you in any of them." Freddy kissed her hands. "You were the love of my life. You are the love of my life, Margo." He sat back again and finished his beer. With the drinks at Sheila's, and the couple at his hotel he felt a little tipsy. "Then Gabrielle got pregnant with Marguerite and . . ." his voice trailed off.

"Gabrielle is stunning," Margo said. "Who could blame you for falling in love with her?"

"I'm not sure I ever was," Freddy confessed. "I mean in love with Gabrielle. Not sure if she was in love with me either. I said we needed each other and maybe that masqueraded as loving each other. Till death do us part, that sort of thing."

Margo removed his plate and rinsed it in the sink. Then she turned around and leaned against the sink, crossing her arms.

"I had to let go of you the best I could," Freddy continued. "It wasn't easy. You were in my blood. You were in the air I breathed. You centered me, Margo. Then I heard about you and Howard and that shredded my insides. At first, I couldn't believe it. You were my Margo. You were my love. And then you were someone else's." Freddy stopped and squeezed his temples. His head pounded. "Painfully, I had to admit to myself that I lost you."

Margo brought him a slice of Black Forrest torte. "Your favorite," she said. "Little Margo's recipe."

Freddy took a bite and then closed his eyes, savoring the kaleidoscope of flavors in the cake. "Sugar, the grub's fantastic. Howard was lucky."

Margo nodded her thanks and thought a minute. Then she said, "Howard was there and he loved me enough to let me keep a corner of my heart for you. Poor dear bore it in silence, and I felt so guilty about it."

"Howie was a saint. If there had to be someone else for you, I'm glad it was Howie. But it still hurt."

"Howard kept a smile on till the end," Margo said.

Freddy took a few bites of the cake and then returned to the kitchen window and again stood looking out and into his life. That night in New Orleans his parents didn't come home. Around dawn his nanny woke him up as he curled up in the window seat and said a nice policeman wanted to talk with him. That afternoon Freddy's uncle Dennis flew in from Chicago and helped him pack a suitcase and said that he was going to live with him in Chicago.

Margo joined Freddy at the window. "Marriages don't fall apart just like that."

"No, they don't," Freddy said, breaking away from his thoughts. "It was a gradual explosion. There was the affair with the film director, and I know there are more. So how do you handle that reality? I should have left, and would have were it not for Marguerite." Freddy paused and turned away from Margo. "Then I stepped out of line myself."

Margo was quiet for a time before saying, "You must be proud of yourself, Freddy. What were you trying to do, get even with Gabrielle? I don't know the woman and can't comment on her behavior. But you disappoint me."

"I disappoint myself."

"So that okays everything?"

"No, it doesn't, Margo," Freddy said, "and I can't forgive myself. Gabrielle can't forgive me, even though she herself had . . . Gabrielle still hasn't forgiven her mother for her alcoholism and abuse and her father for his suicide."

Margo placed a hand on Freddy's shoulder and said, "I think it's time for you to wake up from all these nightmares."

Freddy took her in his arms. "I don't know how, Margo. Tell me what to do. You were always the sane one. I don't know how much more of this I can take. And there's Marguerite . . ." Freddy drew Margo closer in his arms. His lips ached for hers.

"Freddy, don't," Margo begged. "Please, Freddy, it's not right."

He nodded yes and let her ease out of his arms.

Margo put coffee on. "Go relax in the living room and I'll bring you coffee."

Freddy stretched out on the couch, exhausted and beaten. Later he thought he felt a cover being thrown over him. Then he felt a kiss on his lips, a gentle and long kiss, and he thought he heard Margo whisper, "And you are the love of my life, my beautiful Freddy."

21

"**Y**ou kids look like you've been mud wrestling," Phil snickered. "Did I miss something?"

Sitting facing him in her living room, Margo turned the page on her music stand. "Freddy stayed over."

Phil gave Freddy a puzzled look and then turned to Margo. "I hope you had a good time, little sister."

"He slept on the couch there." Margo pointed with her bow. "Was ready to pass out from exhaustion."

"You mean passed out like a dork," Freddy said. "I lay on the couch for a minute and was out cold."

"I didn't want him driving back to his hotel in that condition." Margo turned another page in her music. "Could just see him falling asleep behind the wheel and . . ."

Phil plucked a note on his cello. "Poor baby. Come over here and let me kiss you."

"Kiss your cello and let's get the show on the road," Freddy barked.

Phil drew his bow on the string and turned to Freddy. "How did the Sheila thing go?"

"I'd say you were missed." Freddy played a few chords. "Talked about you. Call her."

Margo made a face at Phil and then turned to Freddy. "What, you're a matchmaker now? For your information, Sheila spits out men like olive pits."

"Maybe Sheila's not used to the premium stuff." Freddy struck a note on the piano. "Our friend here makes for extra virgin quality."

"Now there goes an association I've been dying to own — olive oil." Phil put an ear to his cello and plucked a string.

Freddy laughed and made a few runs on the keyboard. He was tired and his fingers dragged behind his brain.

"Want to know what the great cellist Pablo Casals said about the cello?" Phil plucked a string.

"Something about the cello being like a beautiful woman who hasn't grown older, but younger with time, slender, more supple, more graceful," Freddy answered.

"I thought I was the only one who knew that quote," Phil said, disappointed.

"Casals was talking about you, Margo," Freddy teased, and turned a page on his music.

"I've improved that much with age, you think?" Margo cooed.

"You two aren't at it again, are you?" Phil threw a suspicious look at Margo and then Freddy. "Freddy, for Christ sake, married and chasing the beautiful widow here."

"Thanks for reminding me I'm a widow," Margo snapped.

"Sorry, kid, didn't mean it that way," Phil stuttered.

"Oh, shut up and play," Margo barked, but then suddenly her eyes filled with tears and she ran into the kitchen crying.

Phil ran after her, apologizing.

"Damn it," Freddy grumbled, tapping his forehead on the piano. "Damn it, damn it, damn it." He slept badly and his head pounded. After breakfast he chatted with Marguerite, but no answer from Gabrielle on the Paris apartment phone or on her mobile. His concern for her was growing. Cancel and fly out to Paris?

When Margo and Phil emerged from the kitchen, Freddy was resting his head on his arm on the piano, his music opened to Piano Trio in C Minor, Op. 70, by Edouard Lao. The Lalo piece was his idea and he argued that hardly anyone played it in concert and that it was breath of the unexpected for the anniversary celebration. The piece also served as a fine warm up for Schubert's "Trout Quintet" that was to close the event Saturday night. The Schubert called for the addition of viola and double bass coming from the student orchestra.

Phil and Margo picked up their instruments and sat looking at Freddy.

"If you children have kissed and made up, time to make music," he said.

"About time we stopped Fartin' around," Phil said.

"I mean, really." Margo smiled and tucked the violin under her chin.

They finished a little past noon when Freddy was satisfied enough with the first rehearsal to call it quits. The concert was Tuesday evening at Paulik Hall at the conservatory, and Freddy wanted one more rehearsal. Thursday night he had a recital at the conservatory. They still had to rehearse "Trout Quintet." In between, Freddy had a string of master classes.

Margo's meatloaf washed down with beer closed Kreutzer Trio's first rehearsal after so many years. Then Freddy drove downtown with Phil.

Phil was silent for a while and then said, "Old buddy, don't you ever get tired of playing?"

"I get tired but never tired of playing," Freddy confessed. "Music's my life and the piano my passion." He reflected for a moment. "Music was Connie and Luke's life, but time ran out on them."

"So you're trying to make up for what they lost, is that it?"

"Who knows? Maybe. Or maybe I just love playing the piano," Freddy said.

Traffic crawled. "Sorry for the comment about you and Margo," Phil said. "Just that I started getting flashbacks from London. It was hard on all of us."

"Gabrielle's driving me crazy and Margo's ripping my insides. I don't know what to do."

"The Freddy I knew always figured out a way."

"Yes well, one look at Margo and I can't figure my way out of a sack. "

Freddy took out a pair of cigars from the case in his pocket and passed one to Phil.

Both lit up.

"And then there's the dearly beloved that we have to consider in all this," Phil said.

"Yes well, the dearly beloved went the way of the lost music score." Freddy drew on the cigar. "The dearly beloved has defeated me so completely."

"Why hang around, then?"

"Because of Marguerite."

"And Gabrielle? Why is she hanging around?"

"Probably feels the same — Marguerite." Freddy studied his cigar. "Gabrielle's mother was abusive and alcoholic, and Gabrielle lost her father to suicide."

Phil nodded. "That'll fry anybody's insides."

"I wake up every morning afraid that Gabrielle will destroy herself," Freddy confessed. "Not a good feeling. And what happens to my little girl, then?"

Freddy pulled in front of the brownstone where Phil was staying with his parents. "What about Sheila?" he said. "I think she's sweet on you, old buddy."

"These days I can use some honey for sure," Phil said, "but we come from two different worlds."

"Maybe so, but there's a lot more woman behind her flash and glitz, Phil. Maybe the key to your happiness. I have a good feeling about this one."

"Should I call her?"

"Sure. Could be you're what Sheila needs."

"Yeah, I know, extra virgin olive oil."

"Aphrodisiac for the soul, brother," Freddy said.

22

An awful lot of money made up the conservatory's board of directors now sitting at George Paulik's dinner table. It was no surprise, then, to hear him announce the addition of a new wing to the conservatory with the board's hearty approval. What did surprise Freddy, though, was Paulik announcing the creation of the Frederick Priestley scholarship in classical and jazz studies. By now Freddy was learning to expect the unexpected from George Paulik and this one was right up there.

"I hope Mister Priestley will forgive this old man for not mentioning the honor to him prior to the announcement," Paulik explained. He pointed to the board members at the table. "We thought a little surprise would spice things up."

Later Freddy sat looking into the garden and wondering what else the old fox had up his sleeve for him when Sheila touched his shoulder. "I see you've found yourself another window," she said. "Balconies, windows, all the same." Sheila wore an elegant dress, black, lowcut against her creamy skin. Freddy thought she looked radiant.

"Reminds me of a Viennese garden where you can lose yourself in Mozart and Beethoven," Freddy said, and rose from his seat.

"You must like losing yourself in such places." Sheila came around to face him.

"Sometimes they're the best places for escape."

"George and his music cronies, the quartet, play out there on pleasant summer afternoons," Sheila said.

"Margo's quartet, you mean."

"Yes, Margo's," Sheila said. "She's first violin, George second, the violist is a doctor and the cellist a judge. Margo is the only professional."

"A superb violinist, our Margo."

"Yes, she is," Sheila agreed, "and George says she cracks the whip. By the way, where is Margo? And Phil?"

Margo had some school event going on with the kids, Freddy explained, and Phil a previous engagement he couldn't break. "But if my old buddy knew you'd look this stunning," Freddy added, "he'd have broken a date with the queen and catapulted himself here."

"That's so sweet, thank you." Sheila looked out into the garden again. "So charming and intimate, don't you think? It's George's corner of paradise."

"When our trio started, we had a gig on Sunday afternoons in a Viennese-style garden, a nice imitation." Freddy motioned for Sheila to join him. "A charming place. Oh, what a grand time it was."

"Such sweet memories make life wonderful." Sheila sank in the chair across.

"Yes, sweet," Freddy said. "We were young. Music felt good. And we sent the crowd whistling to Cairo."

"Sent them what?"

"Whistling to Cairo." Freddy laughed. "My mother used to say that to me every time she and my father returned home from playing a gig. Mom did a perfect imitation of Mae West — *'Oh honey, I sent them whistling to Cairo.'*"

Sheila laughed. "That's so charming."

"I mean May West didn't say that specific thing. "Mom just imitated her voice and mannerism."

"What does it mean?"

"I don't really know. Just a saying she had, I guess." Freddy regarded his empty drink.

Sheila asked a server for a refill. "I heard they were performers," Sheila said. "See, I know a lot about you, Freddy."

"So I see." Freddy checked his watch. It was getting late and he was wearing out. "They played cabarets, mostly around New Orleans," he said. "Luke Priestley and Connie Lacourt."

"Would I have heard them?"

"Unfortunately, no," Freddy said. "They didn't record. Perhaps there are tapes of them somewhere." He tried to hide the dew in his eyes and looked away. "They had signed a recording contract and were bringing it home when they were killed — drunk driver."

"I'm so sorry." Sheila reached across and took Freddy's hand. "This is so sad."

Freddy nodded. "Mom had a rapturous voice and she could create the perfect mood with it. It was a small but intimate voice. Pulled you right into it. She was the iconic cabaret singer, and there aren't that many of those. Mom also had impeccable phrasing. And the way Luke's piano floated underneath. It was like a gilded vessel ferrying a queen. Just breathtaking. I was young, but how well I remember."

Freddy fought the dew in his eyes. If Sheila noticed it, she didn't say anything. "What made them exceptional human beings and artists was how much they loved each other," Freddy went on, "and that love was in the soul of their music."

Freddy's drink came and he toasted Sheila.

"You must be in love, too, then," Sheila offered, "because I hear love all over your music."

Freddy took drink and nodded his thanks. He'd had several drinks and they were getting to him.

Sheila studied him. "You know, you have a very beautiful wife. Gabrielle Mersenne is also such a wonderful actress." She watched Freddy take another drink. "Are you terribly in love?"

Long ago Connie said that gentlemen didn't lie, that Luke never did and that there was no grander gentleman than he. So no, no lies.

"Yes, I am," Freddy lied, hoping his mother would forgive him. He checked his watch again. "Too much to drink and rehearsals tomorrow."

Freddy left the reception around midnight. He rolled down the car window and let the cool breeze wash over him. He felt alone. He wanted somebody. He wanted Sheila tonight, and Margo every night. Just to hold somebody. He could not remember the last time he and Gabrielle spent some intimate time together. And he wanted

Gabrielle, but mostly he was worried about her. She was in crazy moods before. Angry, destructive, cruel. This time she scared Freddy.

He lit a cigar and tried to fight the storm in his head. His mobile phone rang.

"I took a chance I'd reach you."

"I'm glad you did, sugar."

"Where are you?"

"Lakeshore Drive, driving to the hotel."

"You sound tired."

"Ready to drop, and a little drunk."

"Not very smart, Freddy," Margo said. "Are you okay to drive?"

"Okay to drive, but not okay otherwise."

"What's wrong?"

"Everything's wrong. Really worried about Gabrielle."

"Why, what's going on?"

"She's in one of her crazy and defiant moods," Freddy said. "They're always dark and explosive. She's liable to do some crazy thing."

"What can you do?"

"Not much, I'm afraid, short of cancelling everything and taking the next flight to Paris."

"Are you really thinking of that?"

"I've done that twice before — cancelled concerts and run to the rescue. All the good that's done me." He took a long puff on his cigar and thought. "Well, let's talk about something else. How are you, sugar?"

There was a long pause and Freddy wondered what Margo was thinking. He could see her rubbing her elbow, the way she always did when mulling over something.

"About last night, Freddy," Margo finally said.

"Loved the meatloaf."

"Thanks. That's not what I wanted to tell you."

"I know."

"Last night I wanted you, too, desperately, but just as well it didn't happen," Margo confessed. "It was wrong. Say it was wrong. Say it, Freddy. I want you to say it."

Freddy could hear his father: "Remember who you are, my little man. You're Frederick Priestley, the son of Luke Priestley, and we have our code of honor, the gentlemen's honor."

Freddy's answer took a while coming. "Yes, it would've been wrong."

"Freddy?"

"Yes, sugar."

Another pause for Margo. "I love you, Freddy," she said. "Oh God, I've never stopped loving you."

Freddy rolled down all the windows. He needed more air to think. "It's more than the two of us involved here, isn't it?" he said after a long pause.

Margo's answer took a while coming. "Yes, more than just the two of us."

"And that's our reality."

"Freddy?"

"Yes, sugar."

"Why wasn't it meant to be for us?"

A gust of wind blew through the windows and chilled Freddy's feverish skin. "And that's my torment," he said.

23

They finished rehearsing at the conservatory around noon. Freddy thought the morning went well, if for no other reason than to be referred to by Margo as "tyrant" only twice rather than a dozen or so times on their first rehearsal at her house. Once during the morning Margo barked, "If I hear 'From the top' one more time, Freddy, I'll run outside screaming and tearing my hair out."

"Tear your clothes off instead," Phil snickered. "Give us something to look at."

"You'll be serving humanity, Margo," Freddy threw in.

"Will you two juveniles pipe down?" Margo said, trying to hide her smile.

"One more time from the top," Freddy announced.

After rehearsal, Margo had to return to her shop. Freddy suggested lunch on the way. He had a master class in the afternoon, and later he needed to practice for his solo recital. Phil didn't feel like writing and planned to hang out downtown.

They ran into Paulik and Sheila outside. Paulik had meetings and left. Freddy suggested Phil take Sheila to lunch and Phil thought it was the best offer he had all morning, especially after putting up with a pair of no-talents.

In the café, Margo sipped her wine and wondered if Sheila can handle an independent soul like Phil.

"She needs a no-nonsense bloke like him."

"How do you know what Sheila needs, pray tell?" Margo gave him a suspicious eye.

"She's a tasty dish, but I think there's a vulnerable side to her that needs someone like Phil."

"Oh, I see," Margo glared at him. "You know I'll kill you if you go near any tasty dish, Frederick Priestley."

"You killed me a long time ago, sugar."

"And don't you forget it."

"Chiseled on my heart forever," Freddy said.

Dew filled Margo's eyes. "Oh God, what are we going to do, Freddy?"

He studied his wine and shook his head. He was all out of answers.

"Every time I walk away from you, I want to cry," Margo said. "It's torture."

"And I've never wanted you more." Freddy regarded her. "This minute."

Margo reached across the table and let Freddy take her hands.

"At least let me take you to dinner after you finish work," Freddy said.

"We're open late tonight and we'll be busy."

"Afterwards, then?"

"The children," Margo reminded Freddy. "I have them in my life, too, and I should be home."

"Yes, of course."

"Come home for a late dinner," Margo offered. "The kids would love to meet you."

Freddy thought a moment. "How much do they know about me?"

"Not much."

"Just as well," he said. "Maybe another time."

"Are you angry with me?"

"No, sugar, not with you," Freddy said. "With life."

After walking Margo back to her shop, Freddy stopped at his hotel for a short nap. First, he called Gabrielle on her mobile and to his surprise she answered. "Where have you been?" he said. "I've been calling you afraid something happened to you."

"I was in the country with a friend," Gabrielle challenged him. "I had a lovely time."

"I'm ecstatic you had a lovely time." There were voices in the background. "Who was your friend?"

"A friend." Gabrielle was defiant.

"Like that answers my question," Freddy said. "You had me worried."

"Why do you care?" Her voice broke.

"Because you're my wife and I worry about you."

"Worry about your girlfriend."

"Will you stop this?" Freddy pleaded. "Stop whatever it is you're doing."

"Are you finished?"

"Finished what?"

"Giving me commands like Napoleon Bonaparte," she shouted. "I have my own life, can't you understand? And you have yours."

Freddy dropped on the edge of the bed and tried to find something to say. Gabrielle beat him to it with a bombshell.

"I'm pregnant."

Reality took a few moments to sink in. Freddy tried to remember the last time they had slept in the same bed and drew a blank. "Who's the father?" he said, pouring himself a drink and trying to stay calm. No easy task for him when trying to deal with Gabrielle on the warpath.

"Someone," Gabrielle sassed.

"Who someone, damn it?"

"Not Napoleon Bonaparte." Gabrielle laughed.

Freddy checked his watch. So much for his nap, and he had a master class breathing down his neck. "Am I to congratulate you?" he said.

"A divorce is enough," she said defiantly.

For an instant Freddy thought he misunderstood Gabrielle, but soon reality slapped him. Yes, divorce. Suddenly scenes of their life together flashed before him, the good and the bad. Then he saw Marguerite's face. Damn the rest, he told himself, what happens to Marguerite? He didn't even want to think about that.

After a time, Freddy said, "Gabrielle, you know what divorce means? This is not a movie role."

"I'm a good actor, Freddy, but not that good."

"Then what happens to Marguerite? You remember her, don't you?"

"I don't care, damn you," Gabrielle shouted.

"My God, do you know what you're saying?" No, she didn't, he was sure. She was out of it. Gabrielle was angry and she was striking out. She was hurt.

"I don't care, I don't care, I don't care." Gabrielle was hysterical.

Freddy felt helpless. Everything was spinning out of control. For God's sake, Gabrielle loved Marguerite.

"Gabrielle, please don't talk like that," he said. "I beg of you. This isn't you. It's something dark inside you that's exploded and we need to deal with it. Please be sensible."

Gabrielle was not listening. "I must go now," she said, calm and sassy. "I have friends waiting, and I'm sure you have friends."

"Sure, they're hanging from the chandeliers."

"Hang yourself from the bloody chandeliers," Gabrielle hissed. "Go play with your girlfriend."

Freddy stared into his empty whiskey glass. It was a while before he realized that Gabrielle was gone and the phone beeping. He hung up and reached for the bottle, but stopped. He then grabbed his coat and fedora and fled his hotel room.

Later, surrounded by young musicians eager to learn from the great pianist, Freddy was not sure how he made it to the conservatory; by what mode of transportation. Had he walked or taken a taxi? Not that it made any difference how he got there, but some things were good to know for his peace of mind.

Gabrielle ripped his heart out. Jammed her fist inside his chest and ripped out his heart without mercy. The pain killed him. He was angry with her, and at the same time frightened for her. He was helpless to do anything while thousands of miles away. Gabrielle was drowning in her private universe and he was locked out.

After class and then some time at the piano practicing for his recital, Freddy spent the rest of the evening wandering downtown. He thought of stopping to see Margo, but he was in no mood for company, even Margo's. Nor did he want to run into anyone he might know.

Quiet was all he wanted. A little bit of peace. After a light dinner in a quiet café on Rush Street, he strolled back to his hotel.

Later, he sat looking out onto Lake Michigan. He was exhausted. Destroyed. He thought he heard Margo say, "My God, Freddy, what have you done to yourself?"

Then he felt Marguerite's arms around his neck and her little voice murmuring, "Goodnight, my beautiful Daddy, I love you," and that was enough to numb his pain.

24

Freddy thought Joe Kline easily passed for an NBA player. He was tall and lanky and a perfect match for his string bass. Joe had a ready smile and an unhurried air about him that Freddy especially liked. Roberta Davis, Robbie, had a pretty face, if a wee bit tight, Freddy thought, and straight hair that fell half way down her back. And so polite.

When everyone was ready, Freddy announced, "Shall we do it, children?"

"Yes, professor Priestley," Robbie said, and tucked the viola under her chin.

Margo made a face at Phil and he snickered.

"All I need now is a beret, thick glasses and a pipe," Freddy beamed. "Freddy the scholar. OY!"

"You'll look awfully cute," Margo cooed.

"Look like a Parisian pick pocket," Phil chuckled.

Robbie looked confused.

"Now, my dear Robbie, ignore these two misguided souls," Freddy said, and played a cluster of chords. He smiled. "My friends call me Freddy."

Margo and Phil smiled at Robbie. Joe smiled. Finally, Robbie herself smiled.

"Now, let's rock n' roll," Freddy announced. "Quintet in A-Major for Piano and Strings, Opus 114 'Trout' by Franz Schubert. From the top, *allegro vivace* — whatever that is."

The first rehearsal went well enough to satisfy Freddy. They all had lunch together in the cafeteria. Freddy then put Kreutzer Trio through a quick rehearsal in preparation for that evening's concert. Later, Phil took a cab to his parents' house to work on Freddy's profile. Freddy and Margo walked to her shop; she was staying downtown for the concert and the children were coming on the train.

Freddy invited Margo to change in his hotel suite, but she said the children might frown on that.

"I called you last night in case you'd changed your mind about dinner at the house," she added, "but you must have been cruising main street."

"Wandering the streets aimlessly and not in the mood to socialize," Freddy said.

"What happened?"

"What makes you think something happened?"

"Because I know you, dear one."

Freddy made a face to dismiss the question.

"Freddy, what happened?" Margo persisted.

He shook his head. "Nothing happened."

"Please, Freddy.

"Nothing happened, Margo," he snapped. "Just forget the damn thing." He closed his eyes and squeezed his temples, regretting his harsh tone, and then when he saw Margo's hurt look, he said, "God, I'm sorry, sugar. Too much crap going on in my life and the last thing I want is to get you involved. Forgive me."

Margo nodded yes and looked away. Nothing more was said until they reached *Swan*. Freddy again apologized, but Margo was not listening as she disappeared into the shop without a word.

Back in his hotel room, Freddy answered his messages. He turned down the dinner invitations, but accepted the media interviews. He spoke with Rufus and Effie about the chili dinner Wednesday and promised to bring the gang.

Earlier Freddy called Marguerite, who naturally wanted to hear more about their planned cross-country trip. He loved hearing her excitement. He considered calling Gabrielle, but gave up on the idea. Say what to her? What more than he had? Mozart wrote that his grandfather said to talk well and eloquently was a great art, but that an equally great one was to know when to stop. So maybe it was said in a different context, but what the hell, it made sense to Freddy in almost any context.

Despite all the madness around him, by concert time that evening, Freddy was ready to play. So were Margo and Phil. Freddy felt the trio soared. Never sounded better. In the romance movement of the Lalo, he glanced over at Margo and smiled, the old smile when he knew Kreutzer Trio was making music like the speech of angels, borrowing from Thomas Carlyle. In the finale, Freddy winked at Margo and she responded with a nostalgic smile. Perhaps she, too, felt the same sadness in knowing that she was making a final appearance on stage with Kreutzer Trio. He looked over at Phil and Phil nodded, as if knowing what Freddy was thinking. It was a bittersweet night, but nevertheless, for the last time, Kreutzer Trio sent the crowd whistling to Cairo.

After the concert Freddy dropped off Margo and the children and drove back to his hotel. In the late hour, traffic was light. The cool air rushing through the open windows felt soft on his burning skin.

He switched on the radio and scanned the dial until he heard jazz: Oscar Peterson. "Thank you," he said to himself. His mobile phone rang.

"I couldn't stand it anymore," Margo said. "Please tell me what's wrong."

"Nothing's wrong."

"All right, I will call you every two minutes until you do tell me."

"I don't want to get you involved in this."

"Of course, you do," Margo protested, and Freddy could feel her tears. "Because we share a history."

So then Freddy told her the whole story. He was still talking when he pulled in front of the hotel and had the valet park the car. Upstairs in his suite, he poured a drink and sank in the chair by the window. "And that's that," he concluded. "Now you've heard the sordid adventures of Gabrielle and Freddy."

Margo was silent before she said, "You two should be flogged for making a mockery out of marriage. Your wife sleeps around and so you go out and do the same disgusting thing? It's not a game, Freddy. This is real life. There are commitments and responsibilities."

Freddy meant to avoid that part of his confession to Margo, but it just slipped out. An affair with a Brazilian jazz singer working in Amsterdam started his mess of indiscretions. Freddy happened to drop in the club after playing with the Royal Concertgebouw Orchestra. He was invited to play a set with her quintet. Later Freddy went with her to her hotel.

"It happened, Margo," he tried to explain. "That night I was flying high on the music and had a little too much to drink."

"Were there other women?"

Freddy hesitated. "Yes."

"Just how many?"

"I don't know, Margo. Damn it, I didn't keep track in my little note-book, if that's what you're heading for."

"What a relief."

"Look, I was angry with Gabrielle. Frustrated. Lost in a bloody maze and didn't know which way to go. I was a mess, Margo. I have my regrets."

"How grown up of you, Frederick," Margo hissed. "Did you regret every time you slept with them?"

"I . . ."

"What did you think you were doing?"

"I have nothing to say to that."

"Of course, you don't," Margo kept up her barrage. "Had I been your wife, I would have slapped your disgusting face and thrown you out."

"And I would not have blamed you."

"That's very noble of you," she said.

Freddy poured another drink. He was tired. His life was tiring. "You're angry with me," he said.

"Angry with myself for having a part in all of this sordid stuff," Margo shouted.

"You have nothing to do with this, Margo. Give me a break."

"Everything to do with it, Freddy."

"I'm the one most to blame," he said. "If I concentrated more on being a husband, there would be none of this."

"Or stopped thinking about the old girlfriend," Margo cut him off.

"Margo . . ."

"You come to Chicago where the old girlfriend lives," Margo cut him off again, "and that sparks this whole ugly affair. Now the old lady really has something to scream about. She has the perfect justification for her behavior — a cheating husband."

Freddy never saw or heard Margo in this mood. She was hurt. She was angry.

"Suddenly the wife's the wronged woman," Margo went on, "because the husband, supposedly, is getting it on with the old girlfriend. The Brazilian jazz singer and all the rest of the women are just little trinkets, compared to the old girlfriend, that is." Margo paused again. Freddy could feel her rubbing her elbow. "I swear you people belong in the sewer. I want nothing to do with you, Freddy. You make me sick. Go home."

Freddy's phone choked quiet. He poured his third drink and sat back looking out the window. Suddenly he was getting it from all directions. And he was getting pissed off. Enough was enough.

It wasn't long before the phone rang again: Margo. "I'm sorry, Freddy. I don't know what came over me."

"Frederick Priestley and all of his stinking garbage came over you, that's what. When you deal with sick and disgusting people . . ."

"Stop that kind of talk," Margo cut him off. "You've suffered enough."

"I've made a mess out of my life."

"No, you have not. Stop that."

"Ironic," he said. "You always centered my life. With you, I knew everything would be okay, even in the darkest hours."

He downed his drink, suddenly realizing that the lights over the lake were making faces at him.

25

In the morning they rehearsed "Trout Quintet." Midway through the theme and variation, Freddy slammed the keyboard and barked at Joe, the bassist, "For Christ sake, we're here and you're on the court rebounding."

"Freddy," Margo snapped. "Please, we're all trying our best."

"Well, damn it, your best isn't good enough."

"Freddy, stop," Margo snapped again.

Freddy caught himself and ran a hand through his hair, frustrated, regretting his outburst. "I'm sorry, Joe," he said. "Margo, I'm sorry. Phil, Robbie, I'm sorry. Let's take a break."

In the conservatory courtyard, Margo took Freddy's arm. "What is the matter with you?" she said. "You're acting like a brute and that's not like you."

Freddy shook his head in frustration.

"These kids aren't like Phil and me," Margo went on, "and they don't need to be punished for the turmoil in your private life."

Freddy squeezed his temples. The walls were closing in on him and nowhere to escape. "It's getting to me, Margo," he said. "Everything."

"I know, Freddy, I know." Margo squeezed his arm. "You're drowning. But not here. Frederick Priestley is too much of a professional."

Freddy covered her hand with his. "It was easier in the old days. Or maybe I think it was."

"Some things were."

"Breaking your heart and moving on wasn't."

"We broke each other's heart and tried to move on," Margo said, "and now it's catching up with us."

Again, Freddy apologized to everyone as they prepared to resume the rehearsal.

"There's this story about Toscanini," Freddy said, then. "You know the famous conductor." He then laid down a cluster of chords. "Toscanini was rehearsing when he got pissed off at the orchestra. So, he stopped everything and said, 'After I die, I shall return to earth as the doorkeeper of a bordello and won't let any one of you in.'"

Margo looked over at Phil and both cracked up laughing. Joe and Robbie followed.

"That's better," Freddy said. "Now let's play. Just think sunshine with this Schubert. Think lovely balloons soaring in blue skies."

"And crashing at a yodelers convention," Phil snickered.

"All right, boys and girls, now let's rock n' roll," announced Freddy, satisfied that he had redeemed himself, and gave the downbeat.

They had lunch in the cafeteria. Afterwards Phil had to write, and Joe and Robbie had classes.

Margo and Freddy drank their coffee in the courtyard. They were quiet for a while, and then Margo brushed a hand over Freddy's brow. "What's happening to you? This isn't my Freddy."

"Life is happening and I'm spinning in place." Freddy held her hand and kissed it. "All I need now is to have it trample over my play-ing. Then I might as well hop on Gabrielle's booze and dope wagon."

Margo's eyes bore into him. "And dare look Marguerite in the eye?" She drew close. "Dare look me in the eye and say you love me? Please, Freddy, that's a weak man crying and you're anything but weak."

Freddy wanted to take her in his arms and just hold her, as he often did in the old days. He needed Margo to quiet the storm inside him. He needed her to calm his heart. She always did.

"Do what you need to do this afternoon and then take some time for yourself," Margo said. "Work on a little peace of mind. Promise?"

Freddy had a master class, and he also needed to practice for his recital scheduled the next evening. He nodded yes.

"And you're still taking me for Effie's chili tonight, right?" Margo said.

"Sugar, Effie's chili is a religious experience, and I'm dying to smoke a cigar with Rufus."

Rufus and Effie were always the one steady force in Freddy's life, always there for him, even in the years he lived abroad. Some nights in the old days Effie made up the bed in the extra room and Freddy slept over. Effie made him breakfast, and if he had no classes, he spent the morning at the piano. All that for the price of hug for Effie.

Rufus told her that she was spoiling the boy and then turned around and asked if he needed money. Freddy did not. He played weddings, private parties and receptions. Where he played made no difference as long as he played. The money he made paid for his tuition and expenses. When he had extra money, he stocked Effie's refrigerator. Effie said he need not do that, but Freddy insisted. And he brought her flowers, lots of flowers, and they made her happy.

Tonight when Freddy walked into the house with Margo carrying several bouquets of flowers, Effie was beside herself. She applauded and cheered. She hugged and kissed Margo and Freddy and then scurried about trimming the flowers and putting them in vases. Margo hugged Rufus and then left to help Effie. Freddy gave Rufus a hug and then presented him with a box of cigars. "Real Cubans, Mister Jazz," he said.

"You're spoiling me, boy." Rufus brushed a loving hand over the sealed box. "Now I can say I'm in heaven," he added.

"The best for the world's best tenor sax player." Freddy followed Rufus to the little bar in the corner.

Rufus asked about Phil and Freddy said he was with Sheila. "Been seeing a lot of her," he added, "and I feel it's love."

Rufus nodded, pleased, and poured them drinks. "And what's going on with you and Gabrielle?"

Freddy waved off a hand.

Rufus nodded. "So it's like that, eh?" Rufus never approved of Freddy's marriage to Gabrielle, although he did not try to talk him out of it. "And I see you're still in love with little Missy?"

Freddy hesitated for a moment and then nodded yes.

"Can't say I blame you," Rufus said. "That girl is special."

Freddy took a drink. "Question is, Ruf, what do I do? What would Luke do?"

"Luke would do what was best for his family," Rufus said. "So, think hard, boy."

After dinner Rufus clipped a pair of cigars for them. Freddy lit up and passed his lighter to Rufus. Freddy then talked about his plans for the tribute recording to Connie and Luke, calling the project a son's marveling at his parents' art. He talked about it through the years.

Rufus drew on his cigar. "Frederick Priestley on piano. I like that. You have Luke's heart and soul, boy, and the same golden touch on the piano Luke did."

"And what singer out there has the heart and soul of Connie Lacourt?" Freddy said. "I can name a few great singers, but none bears the essence of Connie."

Rufus studied his cigar and smiled.

"What, Ruf?" Freddy said. "What are you up to?"

Rufus puffed his cigar and let out the smoke slowly. They all waited. "There's your voice," he said, then, and pointed at Effie. "Only singer I know of with Connie's spirit. Effie's the voice you want."

Effie looked shocked, and Margo's mouth opened wide. Freddy's expression sprang from surprise to glee.

"Oh yes," Margo declared, beaming. "Oh, absolutely. Ruf, my love, you're a genius."

Effie finally came out of her state of shock. "Oh honey, I haven't sung except occasionally. I mean I couldn't . . ."

"You would be wonderful, Effie," Margo said.

"But honey, I don't have the name to excite people," Effie said.

"I do, sweetheart," Freddy said, "and we'll build your name up to make you sound like the Queen of Sheba."

"Goodness," Effie chuckled.

"Besides," Freddy went on, "you knew Mom and you were friends. You heard her sing in the clubs. I can't think of anyone else doing justice to her like you. Ruf's never wrong."

"But I can't sing like your mama, Freddy honey."

"I'm not asking you to, sweetheart," Freddy said. "I want you to sing like Effie Lanier, my other Mama, who remembers her friend

Connie Lacourt."

So, it was settled.

Freddy strutted over to the piano and laid down a few chords. Then he played "Sophisticated Lady" and turned to Effie. "All yours, sweetheart," he said.

Effie cleared her throat and moved over to the piano. A few bars into the song and Freddy flashed a smile. Oh yes, he found his singer.

Effie's voice was sweet and velvety, like a late-night liqueur, Freddy thought. He always loved her voice, but this was the first time he actually analyzed it. It was a young voice and a mature voice dressed in an old woman's memories. Her phrasing floated near Connie's, from what Freddy could remember of his mother's singing style.

Freddy segued into "Skylark" and then to "Gentle Rain," Effie floating along with him. In the end, he looked at Rufus and then at Margo. Both were nodding yes. He looked over at Effie, who had tears in her eyes. "I love you, Mama," he said.

26

"Sure you want to do this?" Margo said. "I mean trying to recreate their music adds to the complications in your life."

Freddy rolled down the window in the taxi and let the cool air wash over him. "I'm not trying to recreate Luke and Connie. As a mature musician, I just want to hear what they might have sounded like. I've hungered for that sound. Not a perfect rendition, but just a hint of their sound."

Margo studied him. "And that playlist could also crush you, Freddy. You thought of that? Tortured memories, regrets. Time to let go, dear. Let it rest. Move on."

Freddy kissed her hand. "Not that easy, sugar. Too many ghosts in the house."

"But you've got to. Either that or a life of brooding." Margo nudged closer to Freddy.

"Maybe the recording is what I need for that closure," he said. "Doesn't matter. Must do the recording and damn the consequences."

Margo brushed a hand across his temple. "My poor Freddy, you're going through hell and I don't have the power to pull you out."

Margo's phone rang. Kristen. They chatted for a while and then Margo wished her and Josh goodnight.

"Everything okay?" Freddy asked.

Margo nodded yes. "The kids are sleeping over at my parents'. There's a teachers conference tomorrow and no school."

"Now we can hit the bars and get drunk and have a good time,"

Freddy joked.

"I have a better idea," Margo said, as the taxi pulled in front of Freddy's hotel to drop him off before taking her home. To his surprise, Margo got off with him. Then she took his hand and led him into the lobby and then to the elevator. "Our room?" she said.

"I'm on the nineteenth floor." Freddy gave her a suspicious look. "Room nineteen-seventeen."

"Vintage year."

"Not for Mata Hari it wasn't."

"What happened?"

"Firing squad, in France."

"Oh."

Freddy took Margo's arm and stopped. "Do you know what you're doing?"

"Not when it comes to you." Tears swelled in her eyes. "The only thing I'm sure of is if you don't make love to me now, I'll die."

On the elevator, Freddy wrapped her in his arms. She cried. Freddy kissed her brow. He closed his eyes and ran his fingers through her hair, remembering a life left behind long ago. The years were gone. So was their chance for a life together. All gone. He blamed himself for everything, but what difference did that make now? The story was finished and the book closed.

In his suite, he took Margo in his arms. "We'll both wake up in the morning with regret," he warned.

"I don't care," Margo whimpered. "Everything I said about marriage and all that I don't care. All that stupid preaching I don't care. I love you, Freddy. Never stopped loving you. And I want to be with you."

Below on Michigan Avenue, a steady hum of late-night traffic played counterpoint to Margo's rapid breathing. An opaque light filtered into the suite from the downtown high rises, and out over Lake Michigan boat lights sprinkled the black waters like distant nomad fires in a still desert.

For years Freddy made his life among the nomad fires of the musical world, playing from one concert stage to the next. He was at home everywhere and loved every moment. Luke predicted as much:

"You'll always be Frederick Priestley, the great concert pianist, at home on every stage." With Margo in his life after all the years, suddenly Freddy felt the strain of his gypsy life. Something in him was changing so that he no longer could easily douse his campfire and move on to the next.

He squeezed Margo in his arms, gently rocking, and wondered what the morning would bring. Tonight, however, he had no choice in the direction he was heading, as if led by a force he could not control. Both he and Margo had come too far tonight and there was no turning back.

"Is this what we want?" he murmured. "Are we sure, my love?"

Margo nodded against his chest. "I'm not sure of anything, Freddy, and I'm frightened. And I'm desperate for you. Like the only thing I've ever wanted in my life."

Freddy carried her to bed, as he did so often in the old days, his heart doubling rhythm, his mouth aching to devour hers, his hands hungry for her naked body. Long ago, he told her that lusting after her was a habit with him, and that making love to her was standard repertoire in his daydreams. How little had changed, he thought, as he slowly sank in his bed with Margo in his arms.

With Margo lying there and asking for his love, if Freddy gave any thought to Gabrielle, it was only in passing and without guilt. At that moment, all he thought of was Margo's body and Margo's love. She was a part of him, stamped on his soul, from the first moment he saw her at the crazy party when they were at the conservatory.

Freddy's mouth closed in and Margo's lips parted with a heavy breath. "Oh God, kiss me, Freddy," she uttered. The kiss started slowly, gently, as they explored each other's mouth, and it stretched into a minute, a day, a month, a year, a century. Freddy lost all sense of time as he floated on an air of warm mist to a place without beginning or end, a timeless place, the same one that he reached when making love to Margo long ago. He abandoned all the thinking, all the brooding, the past, the future, everything, and let his body take life from Margo's love.

His hands followed the routes they knew, along the way still finding surprises, like something new in Brahms with each hearing.

Margo's responses, and her passion, guided him over new paths, as if she left signposts in case someday life brought her to this point.

Later, much later, when Margo's body shuddered beneath him in a series of pulses and she squeezed him again her, pulling all of him inside her, Freddy heard her whisper, "Oh Freddy, I've missed you so much."

27

reddy slept late Thursday, the day of his recital, and when he woke up, lingering notes of lavender and rose teased his senses. Most of all, a night with Margo left him with the sense of gorging love after starvation.

He turned his head, hoping to find Margo lying beside him, but she was gone. He buried his face in her pillow, aching for her lips, for her body. He wanted to make love to her over and over again as if his life depended on it. He felt the same hunger for her after they made love for the first time long ago, and that hunger persisted for days until they made love again. In the end, Margo became a narcotic that Freddy had to have.

So then nothing had change in how he felt about Margo. How much he loved Margo. Looking back now, Freddy realized that he tried to recreate the magic he and Margo had in his marriage with Gabrielle and failed miserably. Any normal person would have known that Gabrielle was not Margo. What was he thinking?

The damn broke the moment he saw Margo in Chicago after so many years of being apart. All that time being away from her he fought to keep his equilibrium. Then in an instant he lost it after he saw her. Suddenly he was transported in time to the night of the party, the night he fell in love with her instantly. Madly in love — just like that.

Freddy remembered thinking the night of the party that Luke would slap his knee and growl, "That's the way we Priestley boys fall in love." Luke fell in love with Connie in one look, and in that moment, she became the love of his life. Like father like son, indeed.

Margo left Freddy a note on her pillow: "It was a wonderful dream, my love, the best I've had in oh so long. I don't know where all this goes, or what will happen. For now, I love you. Your Margo."

Freddy felt another rush of guilt for being unfair to Gabrielle. Even though last night with Margo happened and he would not change a moment of it, he was still married to Gabrielle. She may have wanted a divorce, but that changed nothing in his view, not at this moment, anyway. Despite everything, he still loved Gabrielle, but did she love him? He doubted that. Regardless, the divorce would open the door for Gabrielle to destroy herself. He was terrified.

Freddy showered and took his time shaving. He ate his breakfast by the window in his hotel suite. In the distance Lake Michigan stood calm and clear, blue like Grecian tapestry, blue like Margo's eyes, especially when she wrapped her arms around his neck and said, "I'll die if you don't' kiss me, Freddy."

Sometimes Freddy thought his life began at that conservatory party, at the moment Margo walked into the kitchen and spoke to him. He drove her home in his Aurore after the party, and at the door she turned around and said, "Don't think I do this with just anybody, but I'll die if you don't kiss me goodnight, Frederick Priestley."

They made love three weeks later, in a tiny conference room at her parents' country club. "I'll die if we're caught," Margo murmured before they ripped the clothes off of each other, "but I'll suffer a worst fate if you don't make love to me."

Freddy's mobile phone startled him out of his thoughts. It was Margo, and he answered, "This is the dream factory."

"Sweet dreams, I hope," Margo played along.

"Oh sugar, the sweetest."

There was silence, and then, "Freddy?"

"Yes, sugar."

More silence. Freddy could almost see Margo rubbing her elbow and thinking what she was going to say next. "I lost it last night," she confessed finally. "I lost it and I'm sorry."

"We both did, Margo, but I'm not sorry. Feeling guilty, yes, but not sorry."

"I feel like such a home wrecker?"

"You wouldn't know how," Freddy assured her, recalling Effie's comments long ago, that his young lady possessed such a rich air of goodness about her. "Besides, my home was wrecked before you came back into my life."

"Then I can keep on loving you without feeling guilty?" Margo said.

"You mean now that Gabrielle wants a divorce?"

"That sounds so harsh."

"Reality, remember?" Freddy said. "But let's not think about it for now. Let me take you out to lunch."

"I'd love that, dear," Margo said.

After Freddy hung up, he telephoned Marguerite. She made him laugh, and then smacked a good luck kiss for him for his recital. He called Gabrielle on her mobile phone, hoping to find her calmed down, but there was no answer. He didn't bother leaving a message. What was left to talk about? Gabrielle wanted a divorce and there was no changing her mind. Freddy lived with her long enough to know. It was much in the way she committed to a film role: she stormed into it and kept her focus until the final "Cut."

All this stuff breathing down his neck and with a recital later on. Freddy had a television interview that morning. On the way out he ran into Phil in the hotel lobby. Sheila had a function there, Phil explained, and he just dropped her off.

"Keep me company, then, old buddy," Freddy said. "We ride in class today compliment of the TV station."

"Not every day I get to ride in a limousine."

"A killer journalist like you?"

"Yeah, but who gives an owl's hoot about insuring my little old hands?"

"Ah, but what a brilliant mind."

"You got something there," Phil snickered.

In the limo Freddy clipped a pair of cigars and passed one to Phil.

"You look happy, old buddy," Freddy said, "and you've got love in your eyes."

Phil lit his cigar. "Ah yes. Couldn't have fallen any harder for the stunning Sheila."

Freddy remembered Phil had almost the same look in his eyes when he fell in love with a flutist in Amsterdam. Kreutzer trio was performing there that week and Phil met her at a post-concert party. For the next two days there was no sign of Phil, only to have him show up at the train station dragging his cello and suitcase. The trio had concerts in Prague and then Vienna. The long distant relationship, however, lasted only three months and in the end Phil was heartbroken.

Freddy sank back in the seat and took a long puff on his cigar. "And don't forget the fancy society monogram on Sheila's ass," he said, "and she's also loaded."

"I'll take her ass, but you can keep the monogram," Phil said. "When did we ever give a damn about monograms?"

"And no stiff ass butler is going to show us the backdoor," Freddy recited their old banner as a pair of hotshot musicians and Romeos.

Phil smoked his cigar and nodded. "God, I miss those days at the conservatory. They were sweet days without a care in the world. Just play the music."

"Then we had to grow up and make a mess out of everything."

"Sheila said something like that."

"You're her hero, son," Freddy said. "So, now what happens?"

Phil shrugged. "I guess I'll be staying on. I can write in Chicago as well as in New York. Have to make arrangements to see my boys. That's going to be the hard part of this whole thing, but we'll take it a chapter at a time."

Following the television interview, the limo dropped Phil off at Sheila's and Freddy at Margo's shop. George Paulik planned a celebration dinner for everyone at a local restaurant after Freddy's recital.

Freddy waited at the shop until Margo could get away and then took her to the same Italian restaurant they had been to several times. The waiter called them by name and gave them the same corner booth.

"I wonder what he thinks about us?" Margo said.

Freddy took her hands across the table. "Probably thinks we're lovers or something. Let's ask him."

"I don't think you need the publicity, my love," Margo said.

They ordered salads and wine.

Margo was quiet for a long time. Then she said, "Tell me what to do, Freddy."

"Wish I could, sugar."

"I have a life here, " Margo confessed. "Children. Parents. Friends. My shop. Everything I need is here, everything except you. And you're leaving next week."

"Must go, sugar. Bunch of concerts in Vienna, Prague, Moscow and a few other places."

"So, then what do I do, wait for your return engagement?"

"What are you saying?"

"Just wondering, Freddy." Margo shrugged. "This isn't something I do every day, like opening and closing my shop. Just tell me what to do."

If only the voices in his head had the answers, Freddy thought. "We can't have the years back, Margo, and right now the future with Gabrielle looks bleak." He studied his wine. "I will not give you up again. No matter what happens and who gets hurt." He stopped and shook his head. "What am I saying?"

Margo reached over and took his hands now. "You couldn't hurt Marguerite or Gabrielle any more than give a bad performance."

Freddy kissed her hands and then sank back in the booth. He squeezed his temples. "I'm so tired."

Margo regarded him. "Let's not talk about it now. Have lunch and then get ready for the recital, because honey, you want to send them whistling to Cairo."

"Ah, you remember," Freddy said.

After lunch Freddy washed everything out of his mind except his recital. Later, moments before his performance, he asked the stage director how the house looked and was told the place was packed.

"Don't these people have anything else to do?" Freddy said.

"They're here for the great Frederick Priestley, Maestro," said the stage director.

"Thanks, my friend, but they've wasted their money," Freddy said. "Reminds of a story about the legendary pianist Josef Hoffman."

The stagehand listened, one eye on the clock.

"Hoffman is giving a recital," Freddy began, "and the doorman at the concert hall stops this guy from going in. The guy's crocked. Stone drunk. 'Can't let you in,' says the doorman, and the drunk says, 'Look here, you don't suppose I would go to a piano recital unless I was drunk.'"

They laughed.

"Okay, now let's rock n' roll," Freddy announced, then, and came on stage to resounding applause.

28

"Freddy, darling, you were sensational," Margo said when the crowd of friends and media finally left the dressing room. She kissed him on the cheek. "I mean, you really sent them whistling to Cairo."

"Thanks, sugar," Freddy said. "It felt good." He wanted to squeeze her in his arms and say it felt good because she was there in the audience. Instead, he said, "Now, if you let me take you out for a drink someplace nice, we can make it a big celebration."

"That's very sweet, Freddy dear, but we have a commitment."

"We do?"

"Dinner with George Paulik, remember?"

Freddy made a sour face. He had forgotten.

"And then little Margo must trundle on home to tend her flock," she added.

Freddy thought a moment. "Then make room for us tomorrow. Spend the day with me. We'll drive up north and go apple picking or something."

"I don't think it's apple picking season, dear."

"So, we'll pick something else."

"Don't you have classes at the conservatory?"

Freddy grinned and shook his head. "No classes, no concert, no nothing. Forget apple picking. We'll drive to Lake Geneva and have fish fry."

Margo rolled her eyes, giving in.

"And then we can find a place to be alone," Freddy said. "Just the two of us."

Margo put down her champagne and looked away.

"What's wrong, sugar?"

She turned back to him. "And what, hold hands in Happy Snooze or some other motel? Is that how it's going to be with us from now on, Freddy, an hour here, a half hour there, making love in motel kingdom?"

"Motel here or rowboat on the Yangtze, I don't care as long as I have you in my arms," Freddy snapped.

"But we can't live like that, love like that, in little bits and pieces."

"I'd settle for crumbs rather than starve."

"Think about what you're saying, Freddy. Others are also involved, as you've said."

He downed his champagne and poured himself another one. "I'm tired of thinking," he snapped. "I've been thinking since my parents died. I don't want to think any more, damn it. Sick of thinking."

"Alright, Alright, Freddy, we'll find a way," Margo said, trying to placate him long enough to cool his temper. She did that in the old days.

"We tried to find a way the one time that really mattered most and flunked out — on a Sunday at Heathrow," Freddy said. "We gave up and walked away from each other."

"And the world died a horrible death for me," Margo followed.

Freddy made a sour face at the champagne, thinking he could use a Jack Daniels. "At least I can drive you home after the Paulik thing and we can park somewhere and neck," Freddy said.

Margo laughed. "Do they still do that?"

"Oh, I hope so," Freddy said.

They took a taxi to the restaurant. To Freddy's surprise, Phil and Sheila were there. So were Rufus and Effie. Freddy was under the impression that the Paulik dinner was just for the three of them, but he was happy to see the gang there, anyway. Surprised, that's all. He looked at Margo, puzzled, and she blushed.

"I thought we would make this a family affair and have everyone here," Paulik announced, noticing Freddy's surprised look.

"My family, indeed," Freddy said. He hugged Rufus and Effie, and then Phil and Sheila. Margo followed. Freddy shook hands with George Paulik, suspicious the old fox was up to something. He had already ambushed him twice: first by convincing him to come to Chicago for the celebration, and then for the scholarship.

Dinner was lavish and the conversation light and engaging. When the cognac came, Paulik toasted Margo and Phil for their part in the anniversary celebration, Sheila and Rufus for their help in planning the event, and Effie for keeping Rufus in line. Then he turned to Freddy: "You've done us proud, son, and I'd give anything to be in your shoes. My Lord, the way you make the piano sing. If I could only do that with my violin."

Freddy held up his glass and nodded his thanks. "The great Johann Sebastian Bach thought there was nothing wonderful about playing the organ. He said he struck the right note at the right moment and the organ did the rest. In my case it's the piano," Freddy concluded.

"Such refreshing modesty," Paulik said. He then produced a box of Montecristos and passed it around. Freddy, Phil and Rufus helped themselves. Paulik lit his cigar and drank his cognac. "And that opens several avenues for the conservatory," he said finally.

Everyone at the table waited. Freddy lit his cigar and passed his lighter to Rufus.

Paulik looked around the table. "We have already established the Frederick Priestley scholarship for needy students at Chicago Conservatory of Music," he announced, looking at Freddy. "We are very proud of you, son. Now, I'm wondering . . ." Paulik stopped and looked around the table. "I'm wondering if we could also have the honor of your talent and gilded name on our faculty."

Did the old fox ambush him again? The third time? A knot tied in Freddy's stomach and he felt the irritation. He threw a furtive glance around the table and received no response from anyone.

"I've asked for their strictest confidence and everyone has been kind enough to indulge an old man," Paulik explained sensing Freddy surprise and irritation.

Old man, my ass, Freddy grumbled to himself. "Surely you don't expect me to take a big slice out of my concert life and become a school teacher?"

"Heavens, no," Paulik was quick to respond. "That would be a trag-edy of epic proportion. The world needs you and your music, son."

"Thank you, sir," Freddy said. He threw a critical eye at Margo, dis-appointed in her for not warning him, especially since she knew how he felt about the trappings of formal teaching. Not only that, but with everything else going on in his life, teaching was something he didn't need. Margo blushed and looked down.

"Your alma mater needs you, son," Paulik continued. "In any way you see fit. Other virtuosi have joined music schools around the world, in one way or another. We very much want you before another school knocks on your door."

Freddy tried to temper his irritation, not only at Paulik, but every-one else around the table, and especially Margo. "Others have," he shot back at Paulik, "and I've made sure not to be home."

Paulik looked around the table, his eyes stopping at Margo, as if telegraphing her relationship with Freddy. All eyes turned to her. She blushed.

"Perhaps we at the conservatory can do more to convince you," Paulik said.

"Thank you for the offer, Mister Paulik," Freddy said, "except that I wasn't cut out to be a school teacher."

"On the contrary, son, you've nailed it," Paulik kept on. "A natural. Students love you."

The old fox was rubbing it on thick, Freddy thought, but he also had to admit to himself that thus far he was enjoying his master class-es. "I did things the way my professors had, and especially Rufus. So, I guess it comes naturally."

"There you go," Paulik said, confident. He looked around the table and everyone nodded. Margo sat frozen. Paulik offered a toast and everyone followed. Margo took her time joining in the toast, her eyes nowhere in Freddy's direction. "And another thing," Paulik added, "you have a big family in Chicago. It's home. Just look around you, son. You're loved."

Perhaps Paulik knew about what was happening with Gabrielle. Margo would not have told him, Freddy was confident, but there was a good reason Paulik was who he was. Freddy couldn't help but like the old fox. It was obvious to Freddy that the old man was insinuating a move to Chicago. That's all Freddy needed. He could just see Gabrielle hearing that request, even though she planned to adios the marriage.

"My home is in London, Mister Paulik," Freddy said. "My daughter." He hesitated. "My wife. You don't expect me to . . ."

"No, no," Paulik intercepted Freddy, waving off a hand. "The world is the great Frederick Priestley's home."

Sure it is, you old buzzard, Freddy grumbled to himself. The sly old bandit had more tricks up his sleeve than a band of gypsies. "I'll give it some thought," Freddy said in the end, and glanced over at Margo, who blushed and looked away.

29

After the George Paulik ambush Freddy and Margo walked to Freddy's hotel and from there Freddy drove her home. Both were silent for a time. Freddy was angry with her. No, not angry. He could never be angry with Margo. Just irritated that she did not warn him about Paulik.

Despite all that, Freddy was sure that if he could live anywhere in the world at that moment, he would choose the little space in the car with Margo beside him. He wanted to tell her that, and then stop the car and take her in his arms. Something told him Margo was caught in the same storm, because there was a time when they could read each other's mind.

"If I didn't know you better, you hussy, you were part of the George Paulik ambush," Freddy said instead.

Margo nodded yes. "Are you angry with me I didn't warn you?"

Freddy shook his head no.

"We all had to keep George's confidence," she said. "He's a good man, Freddy. Sly, maybe, but a good man, and a man of his word."

"I know he is," Freddy said, "I like the old buzzard."

"Paulik wants you at the conservatory in the worst way. So does the board. They're all foaming at the mouth to have you and your name connected with the place."

"Paulik is asking the impossible."

"Not even an occasional master class or something?"

"I don't want to think about it now, Margo. I have enough crap going on in my head."

Margo knew Freddy enough not to push the subject. Instead she reached for his free hand. "At least hold my hand, my beautiful Freddy."

Freddy kissed her hand, and again did so at her door when saying goodnight.

The next morning Margo kissed him on the cheek and led him into the kitchen. She wore jeans and a burgundy turtleneck sweater. With her hair in a ponytail, for a moment she took Freddy back to the conservatory days.

"Had breakfast?" she said.

He had.

"Then sit down and have some coffee." She poured him a cup. "You look tired."

"It's all the damn chattering in my head." He took the cup from Margo.

"Call Marguerite?"

"From the hotel, yes," Freddy said. "Gabrielle's flying home from Paris and the two highnesses are going shopping. The kid loves to shop just like her mother."

"Wish you were with them instead of being with the old girlfriend?"

"Are you my girlfriend?"

Margo gave him a vague smile and said nothing.

Freddy sipped his coffee and thought about the phone conversation with Gabrielle the previous evening, after he returned to the hotel. The message from Gabrielle was urgent, and she picked up on the first ring. She sounded calm, loving even, although Freddy heard tears in her voice.

"There is no child," Gabrielle confessed first thing. "I'm not pregnant."

Should he be shocked or angry, Freddy wasn't sure. Gabrielle pulled all sorts of stunts, but this one was way over the top.

"But why . . .?"

"Because you're in Chicago with her," Gabrielle said, "and I wanted to hurt you."

Freddy struggled for words and nothing came out.

"Forgive me, *cheri.*" Gabrielle began to cry. "I love you, Freddy, and I want our life back. I want Steyer back. Remember? We were so happy then."

Yes, they were. Freddy heard it in his recording of "Trout Quintet." Even though leery of Gabrielle's so-called confessions and apologies, Freddy was still willing to give her the benefit of the doubt.

"I love you, Freddy," Gabrielle repeated, and then repeated again.

The conversation stretched late into the night as Gabrielle sketched her plans for their new life. They would go dancing, spend time in *Provence*, where they would drink wine and have lovely food. And they would return to Steyer. And they would make love. "And maybe we can have another child," Gabrielle added. "You think maybe, Freddy?"

Thus far the conversation was full of surprises and the last bit of news left Freddy speechless. Having another child, under the current conditions in their marriage, was insane, he thought, but let the subject pass. They talked a lot more and Gabrielle cried a lot more. Freddy promised to fly back to London after the celebration and there would be plenty more time for them to talk.

"Book a flight to London as soon as you can, Gabrielle, and go home," Freddy added.

"Yes, *cheri,*" she said. "As soon as you hang up."

"Promise me, Gabrielle," Freddy insisted.

"I promise, *cheri,* I promise," she said.

At dawn, tired and sleepy, Freddy called Gabrielle again. She sounded bright and bubbly. She had some shopping to do in Paris before catching a late flight to London. Again, she said she loved him and that she couldn't wait to see him.

After the call, Freddy headed for Margo's with no particular plan for the day but to go for a drive. Go anywhere. Margo asked if he would be disappointed to return in time for the children coming home from school.

"A mother should be home for her children," Freddy said.

"God, how refreshingly old fashioned." Margo poured more coffee.

"Do they know about us? The Children?"

"I think they know something is going on, but I can't be sure."

"And exactly what is going on between us?"

"What, that mommy holds hands with the boyfriend, who happens to be a married man?" Margo's face tightened. "That's about it, isn't it, Freddy? Our reality?"

"You make it sound so harsh, Margo. I'm feeling guilty enough."

"It's the truth."

"The truth with its own realities, yes."

"Which are?"

"That things are more than a matter of black and white, day and night."

"And that's the difference between us, my darling," Margo said, eyeing Freddy tenderly. "I see realities and you . . . you chase butterflies."

"I have a special talent for that," Freddy said, slightly irritated.

"Sorry, darling, that came out wrong."

"It's the truth and you're right," he admitted.

They drove off later, heading north. Freddy fed a compact disc in the player: Robert Schumann's Piano Concerto in A-Minor.

Margo listened intently. "That' not you playing," she said.

"Martha Argerich."

"Oh, I love her."

"So do I," Freddy said. "A wonderful pianist. Love what she does with the Schumann."

"I have your recording of the Schumann and love it best," Margo said. "So romantic. It's you, Freddy."

"You're just prejudiced."

"Don't think so, dear." Margo patted his arm. "No one plays Schumann the way you do."

"Schumann is like a love letter." Freddy blew Margo a kiss.

Margo pulled her coat tighter around her. "Like all the love letters I wrote you and never sent."

Freddy nodded, knowing he wrote her countless letters in his head. "Schumann said that some think music is only intended to tickle the ear, and some treated it like it was some kind of a mathematical calculation." Freddy blew out a breath. "Nah, not so for Schumann himself. For Schumann, music was the ideal language of the soul."

"That's you, Freddy, and that's what I've always loved about you," Margo said. "I've never known anyone who loved music as much as you do. You love it heart and soul."

Freddy turned and flashed her a loving smile. "Ah, sugar, what you do to me." He opened and window and lit a cigar. The cool air felt good.

"Sometimes I used to see us as Robert Schumann and his wife Clara Wieck Schumann. She was a glorious pianist in her own right. The first time Robert saw her, though, he didn't think she was the coolest looking chick in the neighborhood."

"Is that what you thought the first time you saw me?"

"I was too much in love to think the instant I saw you," Freddy recalled. "My God, you made everything freeze in place around me."

"There were plenty of other girls at the party and you had a reputation," Margo reminded him.

"I only saw you, sugar."

Margo rubbed her elbow. "Do I still take your breath away?"

Freddy thought his smile said everything she wanted to hear.

"You still take my breath away, you know?" Margo said.

Freddy blew her a kiss and turned his eyes back to the road. "The first time Schumann kissed Clara was when she was sixteen or so."

Margo sighed. "I was a little older when you first kissed me. Remember? We were saying goodnight at the door after you drove me home from the party. Except that I asked you to kiss me."

"It was a lovely kiss and it lasted forever."

"I still taste that kiss." Margo rubbed her elbow. "Do you still love me the way you did once upon a time?"

"Maybe even more, if that's possible," Freddy nodded, guilt clawing at him.

30

The old café now sported a fancy Espresso machine and other accoutrements of a modern coffee shop. The seating was about the same, though, and they sat at their old table. Freddy suggested a light lunch. He planned to take Margo and the kids out for a big Italian dinner. "We'll have mounds of spaghetti and wash it down with a fine Chianti," Freddy offered.

"You'll conquer Josh's heart with the spaghetti," Margo said, "but Kristin is at a prissy stage, and I swear sometimes I'm tempted to feed her dogfood."

"Don't tell me I have to worry about that with Marguerite." Freddy winced.

"Hold on to your chapeau, dear," Margo warned.

They had lunch, Margo a salad and Freddy a small sandwich. They talked about music and the places Freddy had played. Then Margo popped the question Freddy expected sooner or later.

"Do you still love Gabrielle?" she said.

Freddy studied his coffee before answering. "Yes, I still do love her. She's my wife and Marguerite's mother. There are lingering memories, moments, feelings. You can't toss them out like yesterday's leftovers, despite our marital difficulties."

Margo said nothing and looked away.

"And Gabrielle's looks can make you go weak at the knees," Freddy added, and immediately regretted the comment. "Sorry, sugar, I didn't mean to . . ."

"That's all right, Freddy." Margo faced him and held up a hand to stop. "I get the picture. After all, Gabrielle is stunning and you're a man."

The conversation was heading into a troubling storm and that was the last thing Freddy wanted. "I thought we promised not to talk about things like that today," he said.

"And think about them," Margo followed, "but I keep looking into my crystal ball and seeing trouble ahead."

"Barely hanging on myself," Freddy said. "My lifeline is snapping a strand at a time and I don't see a rescue boat." He picked up his sandwich and proceeded to remove the alfalfa sprouts, grumbling, "For heaven's sake, alfalfa sprouts? That's all I need."

Margo smiled, knowing how much he hated alfalfa sprouts.

"I don't know what the future holds, Margo," Freddy said, satisfied he had removed all the alfalfa sprouts, "but not having you in my life is not an option. Where that leaves us, I don't know."

Tears filled Margo's eyes.

"I'm sorry, sugar. Didn't mean to make you cry." Freddy gave her his handkerchief. "Not that you haven't done enough crying already. When I think of all the pain I've caused you . . ."

"I had a big part in that, too, don't forget." Margo took his handkerchief and wiped her tears. "Sometimes . . . Sometimes I wish you had stayed away," she said in a halting voice. "I wish Paulik hadn't called you. I wish . . ."

"Do you really mean that?" Freddy said.

Margo shook her head no. "Who am I kidding? The past few days together have thrown me my own lifeline. I don't want it snapped again. Not twice in my lifetime."

They talked a lot more, and when they left the coffee shop, it was close to the time the children would be home from school. Freddy fed a CD in the player.

"Schumann," Margo said after listening.

"*Kinderszenen*" — "Scenes of Childhood."

"That's you playing," Margo said. "Love your interpretation." She paused. "I just love you, Freddy."

Freddy winked at her and smiled. "Did I tell you the one about

Schumann?" he said, then.

Margo pulled her coat up to her chin. "I can't wait, dear."

"This woman walks up to the pianist at the party after the concert," Freddy started. "She's gushing like a debutante. Says she really enjoyed that last encore he played. Says she must know what the piece is, because she wants to buy the music for her little daughter to learn it. The pianist says, 'Madam, that music was a piano work by Robert Schumann, Opus Twenty-Three Number Four.' The lady gushes some more and says, 'oh, how wonderful. I just love opuses.'"

Margo tried to hide her laugh and couldn't. "You goofball," she said, "why did I ever fall in love with you?"

Freddy rubbed the back of her neck. "Must have been for the way I play the piano."

"That is only a part of it."

"What's the other part?"

Margo took his hand and placed it over her heart.

Both agreed it was a fine outing, even though they spent all of it at the café, but later, with one quick swipe, Kristen soured their day, shocking Margo and Freddy into reality.

They were getting ready to leave the house for the Italian restaurant when Kristen suddenly stopped and threw an angry look at Freddy. "Are you sleeping with my mother?" she demanded.

If the question shocked Freddy, he felt the explosion it sent through Margo. She froze in the foyer, glaring at Kristen, then at Josh, Freddy next, and then back at Kristen.

"How dare you, young lady?" Margo was furious. "I can't believe you said that."

Kristen turned away from her mother, her chest rising and falling with each heavy breath. "Well . . ."

"You apologize this minute, young lady," Margo cut her off, "and after you do, I want you to disappear in your room."

"I'm not a baby, mother." Kristen was defiant.

"Then you should know the meaning of propriety," Margo now shouted. "How dare you?"

This was the one side of Margo Freddy never saw. Margo not this angry. "It's all right," he said, trying to calm the atmosphere.

"It most certainly is not," Margo fought back. "This is not the daughter I've raised. This is an ill-mannered . . ." She glared at Kristen. "I don't know who this is."

Kristen slowly turned to her mother. "I'm sorry," she said, and then to Freddy, "I'm sorry, Mister Priestley." She then broke into tears and ran upstairs to her room.

Margo looked at Freddy and shrugged. "I don't know what to say. I'm so sorry, Freddy."

Freddy flipped a brow and tossed off a hand. No, this was not something he expected from Margo. Sometimes he still couldn't believe Margo was a mother, not the young girl in the ponytail who asked him at the party if there was anything else to drink besides beer and coke. Not that he blamed Margo for her reaction.

Josh, who was standing quietly in the corner, scratched his head and announced, "This mean spaghetti is out, Mom?"

"Tonight and all other nights," Margo snapped. "I want you in your room, too."

"What did I do?"

"I'm just ashamed of my family and too angry to explain right now."

Josh gave Freddy a pleading look and Freddy shot him a discreet eye signal to disappear before his head ended up on the guillotine.

"Not fair," Josh shouted, shuffling upstairs to his room. "I didn't do anything. Stupid Kristen."

Freddy watched Josh disappear upstairs. "So there you have it," he said to Margo. "It's one of our realities and it doesn't look pretty. No butterflies to chase in this episode."

"I don't know what to say to that, Freddy." Margo was still angry. "These aren't my children. I don't know who they are or where they came from."

"Kristen's missing her father."

"I know that," Margo said. "We all miss Howard. But this behavior is not allowed. Unacceptable, Freddy."

"Kristen looks at me as the stranger trying to take her father's place."

"But that's not so, Freddy."

"I know it's not, but Kristen sees it differently."

Margo rubbed her elbow and said nothing.

"Let's call it a day and I'll see you tomorrow morning at rehearsal," Freddy said.

Margo then kissed his cheek. "My poor Freddy, you're getting it from every direction."

31

Saturday morning Freddy telephoned home. Marguerite came on the line. She was upset. "Mummy promised me a day out for the girls," she said in tears. "We were going shopping, Daddy, and then we were going to have tea and sandwiches at Fortnum and Mason. Mummy didn't come back from Paris."

Nanny told Freddy that she spoke with Madam in the morning and that Madam was flying out later in the day, after some shopping. Freddy assured Marguerite that her mother might have changed to a later flight because of some extra shopping. That calmed down Marguerite.

Freddy called the Paris apartment: "Gabrielle, where are you?" Left the same message on her mobile.

Later in the morning, Margo took his arm and said he looked distant. "I hope it's still not Kristen and what she said."

"Kristen's missing her father and can't accept a fill-in, that's all," Freddy said.

"Still no excuse for her behavior."

"Of course not," Freddy said, "but you can't blame her for wondering what's going on."

"And what is going on, Freddy? Just exactly, what are we?"

He had no answer for her; his mind was on Gabrielle. She disappeared before, sometimes a whole day, sometimes a whole weekend, and by now Freddy knew what to expect: that she finally showed up and acted as if nothing happened. She needed to get away, she explained later, and nothing was said after that.

This time around Freddy felt uneasy with her disappearance. He didn't know why. He called her again before leaving his hotel for rehearsal and left messages on the apartment phone and on her mobile. He was angry with her. She promised him to be home.

Freddy abandoned his thoughts and caught up with Margo, who was saying, "And soon I can hear the gossip going around, something about Frederick Priestley and his mistress Margo Kendrick, or some idiotic thing like that."

"Who gives a damn what people say, or newspapers?" Freddy snapped.

"Unfortunately, I do, Freddy," Margo said. "I live here. My children. Family. Friends. My shop. I guess I'm not as brave as you."

Suddenly Margo, too, was starting to grind him down, like everything else in his life. They were going back and forth over the same terrain and nobody was getting anywhere. He ran a frustrated hand through his hair. "Can we forget this for a while and concentrate on rehearsing?" he grumbled finally.

When a hurt Margo turned to walk away, Freddy grabbed her arm. "I'm sorry, sugar. Please, don't pay attention to me."

"You're not that easy to ignore, Freddy." Margo tried to jerk out of his grip, angry at him.

Freddy held on. "I know, I know, I'm sorry." He pulled her into his arms. "I'm losing it, Margo. Everything's getting away from me and I'm running as fast as I can to catch up."

Margo stayed in his arms.

After rehearsal, Phil took a taxi to Sheila's. Following lunch at the little Italian restaurant, Margo went back to the shop. Freddy returned to his hotel and called Gabrielle again and had to leave a message: "I'm getting worried," he said. He called her again before leaving for the concert and left another pair of messages. Nothing from Gabrielle.

He finally had his answer in his dressing room after the performance that night. Margo found him in the dressing room slumped over the makeup table with his face buried in his hands.

"A fabulous 'Trout Quintet', Freddy," Margo burst with

excitement. "Oh, it felt so good to be playing again like that." When Freddy made no response, she stopped. "Freddy?" She drew closer. "What's wrong, Freddy? What's going on?"

Freddy shook his head without looking up. Margo put a hand on his shoulder and he made no move.

"What is it, darling?" she kept on. Then she saw the message on his mobile phone from the Paris authorities to call as soon as possible. "Oh my God, what's happened?" Still no answer from Freddy. Her voice broke. "You're scaring me, Freddy."

When he finally turned and faced her, Freddy had tears in his eyes and his face was gray, like a death mask. Margo, shocked by what she saw, covered her mouth as if trying to muffle a scream, and stared at him.

"Gabrielle," Freddy choked, barely audible. "She's . . ." He shrugged, confused.

"What's happened?"

"Overdose."

"Oh my God. Is she all right? In the hospital?"

Freddy closed his eyes and squeezed his temples. "She's . . ."

"What? What is it, Freddy?"

"Dead," he said. "Gabrielle is . . . She died. Passed away in Paris sometime today."

Margo's silent scream returned and, covering her mouth again in shock, she sank into a chair close to Freddy. "No, no. Oh God, no, not this, Freddy."

"They found her in the apartment. Friends did. Dead." Freddy stopped and squeezed his temples. "Called the authorities. Overdose, I guess, they thought. Cocaine, alcohol, and God knows what else." Freddy pounded the table with his fist. "Damn it, Gabrielle, why? You promised me."

Margo came over and put a calming hand on Freddy's shoulder.

"They must have called while we were playing the Schubert," Freddy said. "I had my phone in the room here. They left that message. I called them back."

"Freddy, dear, I am so sorry," Margo said, in tears. "This isn't fair. Does Marguerite know?"

Freddy shook his head no. "Told Nanny to keep it to herself until I get home." He thought a moment. "What do I tell Marguerite? How do I explain her mother has died? I don't know. Marguerite was expecting a day out for the girls. To go shopping with her mother."

"Oh, Freddy, how much more pain can you take?"

Freddy suddenly laughed, a sardonic laugh, and then addressing an invisible audience, he announced to the makeup mirror, "Here he's playing footsy with the girlfriend while the little wife's getting herself dead. Pumping enough poison into her to . . . Isn't that hilarious, girlfriend?"

"Not hilarious, Freddy, but tragic," Margo responded, upset with his comment and his tone, "and the way you put it is so cruel. It's not like you."

"Well, I feel cruel," Freddy shouted, and pounded a fist on the makeup table. "And I feel damned."

Margo watched in silence.

"Damn it, Gabrielle, why?" Freddy addressed the mirror again, his tone now softened. "Why did you do it, you stupid, insane . . .? Damn you." He then turned to Margo. "Why would she do such a thing?"

Margo reach over to touch Freddy's face.

"Don't, Margo," he snapped, pulling away from her. "Just don't, please."

"Freddy, darling, listen to me," Margo begged, masking the hurt from his outburst.

He shook his head no. "Please, Margo, not another word. Please."

Phil and Sheila walked in then followed by Paulik. It took Phil only a moment before saying, "What the hell's going on?"

Freddy kept staring into the mirror without answering.

Phil turned to Margo, who was sobbing. "What the hell is going on?" he shouted.

Margo wiped her tears and told them.

Freddy telephoned Rufus and Effie and told them what had happened. A short while later he flew out of Chicago on Paulik's private jet. His tears had dried up and his heart and brain were somewhere beyond his reach. He found himself lying on the battlefield blown to bits, his past, present and future scattered in blood. Then he heard Rufus again: "Hold on, boy. Stay strong. Marguerite needs a father. She needs you. And you need her. Remember that."

32

abrielle Mersenne's sudden death made big news around the world and shocked the film industry. Drugs and alcohol were determined to be the cause of her death. While fans mourned her passing, the tabloids used her for target practice. It hurt Freddy. It was unfair, he thought, and all he could do was to shout at every ugly word written about Gabrielle.

The tabloids also ran suggestive photos of Gabrielle, taken mostly from *Algerian Dawn*, considered by critics to be her worst film. One critic called the film pure porn and unworthy of an esteemed actor such as Gabrielle Mersenne. That hurt Gabrielle the most.

"I begged her not to make the film," Freddy told Margo over lunch in the garden at his home in London. Phil and Sheila had already returned to the U.S. and Margo was flying out the next day. "The script was crap, I said, pure sleaze. Might even hurt her career, I said, but Gabrielle didn't listen." Freddy filled Margo's wine glass and then his. "Sometimes I think she made the film just to spite me," he said, then. "All I want now is for her to rest in peace, something she never had while she lived."

Some of the stories written about Gabrielle made reference to her "estranged husband," the renowned American concert and jazz pianist Frederick Priestley. They dredged up the tragedy in Freddy's life with the death of his parents in a fiery car crash. A New Orleans publication ran an old photo of Luke and Connie playing at a nightclub.

There were photographs of Freddy, too: at the funeral; strolling in Kensington Gardens with Margo and Marguerite; coming out of Harrods with Margo; and dining at a restaurant with Margo. One caption referred to Margo as the "mystery woman" in Frederick Priestley's life. Another called Margo Frederick Priestley's old love.

"Next they'll have us murdering Gabrielle to continue our illicit love affair," Freddy told the gang over cognac at his house. Marguerite was in bed.

"Oh God, Freddy, don't say that," Margo begged.

"Wouldn't put it past the tabloids," Phil said.

Freddy snickered. "I can see the constabulary hauling Margo's ass and mine to the hoosegow."

"Confess Margo did it," Phil joked.

"This isn't funny, you juveniles," Margo grumbled.

Freddy took a pair of cigars from the humidor and passed one to Phil. They both lit up. Freddy sank in the leather recliner and announced, "Now, I have a story for y'all."

"This actor calls on Offenbach. The servant says the composer is dead. Says he died peacefully, without knowing about it. The actor sighs and says he'll be surprised when he finds out."

They laughed before a morbid silence set in.

Gabrielle was buried in a little village outside Paris where she was born. After the funeral, Paulik, Rufus and Effie flew home from Paris in Paulik's private jet. Margo, Sheila and Phil flew to London with Freddy and Marguerite. They all stayed at Freddy's house in Kensington.

"Seems we've been here before," Margo confessed when her flight at Heathrow was announced.

How well Freddy remembered their last goodbye years ago. Afterwards he roamed the streets of London all night, as if losing Margo killed the purpose for his life. "It was a long time ago, Margo," Freddy said, "but now it seems it was like yesterday."

"Will you let me know how you are?" Margo said. "And take care of Marguerite. She's a precious little girl and now she needs you more than ever."

"We'll be fine." Freddy handed Margo her small carry-on bag. "Marguerite is a big girl and she's strong."

"It's you I'm worried about, dear."

Freddy shrugged. "I'll survive. I've canceled all concerts this summer. The recordings, too." He then tossed a hand in the air. "Suddenly I don't feel all that musical."

"You're still doing the cross-country trip back in the states with Marguerite, aren't you?"

"I've promised her."

"Then I'll see you in Chicago," Margo said.

She kissed him on the lips, a small kiss, and he surprised himself by pulling back a little. Margo's eyes betrayed her surprise at his action. Freddy didn't know why he pulled back, even for that small kiss. Margo was his love. Yet he wanted to push her away and say goodbye without touching, as if touching her magnified his part in Gabrielle's death.

Margo regarded him, hurt, and murmured, "Something's happened to us, too, hasn't it?"

Freddy thought a moment. "Not to you, Margo, but I've died inside all over again."

Margo started to walk away, but then turned around. "Gabrielle's death wasn't your fault, you know?" she said. "You feared something like that happening all along. You said it was inevitable. Don't you remember?"

"It's always been my fault," Freddy said. "Look what I did to you."

"You didn't do anything to me. Listen, we both had choices to make and we made them. As you can see, I survived."

Freddy nodded and said nothing. Margo's flight was called again.

"I wonder if there will ever be a time when you can forgive yourself for whatever crimes you seem to think you've committed," Margo said.

Freddy ignored her reasoning. "Gabrielle had needs and I damn didn't see to them."

"And who was going to see to your needs?" Margo's tears welled up. "Who would hold your hand and ask if you needed anything? Who was going to hold you and say you were loved?" Margo shook her head, disappointed, and then walked away without waiting for his answer.

The last people who saw to his needs were Connie and Luke and they were wiped out of his life in a fiery crash when he was 10. That was 30 years ago. The age 35 was a lifetime for Mozart. It was for Luke. Connie's was 31 — Schubert's lifetime. How could Freddy forget?

And now Gabrielle. She died at 35. She was found on the floor leaning against the bed, clutching her mobile phone. The authorities determined she was in the process of dialing — Freddy's mobile phone — and managed only seven digits before losing consciousness.

How could Freddy forget that image and still hold hands with Margo? Gabrielle was trying to reach him. She needed his help and he was thousands of miles away with the old *girlfriend*.

He would never allow Marguerite to suffer as he did all his life. Marguerite lost her mother, but he would be both father and mother to her. So, to hell with his needs. They meant little compared to Marguerite's. Her needs were his main concern now.

33

In the weeks that followed, Freddy spent some time at the piano and the rest he devoted to Marguerite. They ate out a lot, and when at home, Nanny cooked for them. Marguerite practiced her violin and they played duets. Freddy also made sure Marguerite didn't forget her friends.

Some nights Marguerite woke up crying for her Mummy. Freddy knew all about waking up in the night and crying. He held her close and talked about their cross-country trip in America.

"Even if the car's not Daddy's sweet Aurore," she whimpered one night, wiping her tears, "we'll still have a lot of fun driving down the highway, won't we?"

"Just the two of us, sugar." Freddy gave Marguerite a squeeze. She was his lifeline.

Phil phoned from Chicago. He and Sheila were getting married. "I never thought I could love again," he said, "but here I am with my heart doing the mazurka."

The wedding was planned to coincide with his return from the cross-country Trip with Marguerite, Phil told Freddy, and that Margo was helping Sheila with the detail. When Freddy spoke to Margo on the phone, she confessed to her changed perception of Sheila. "Take away the glitzy armor and the demanding ways and Sheila's actually a human being," she admitted. "And she's a knockout. You missed your chance with her, buddy."

"Just as well that I'm stuck on a fiddle playing hussy," Freddy said.

"Are you really stuck on me, Freddy?"

"Like the glue in your fiddle, sugar."

"Is that why you can't bear to be near me?"

"Don't do this to me, Margo," Freddy begged, knowing she was right. "Please not now. I'm trying to survive a storm."

"Because every time I came close to you at the funeral and then in London, you slammed the door in my face, like I had the plague," Margo was not listening.

"Margo, please."

She ignored Freddy again and continued her lament. "Don't you think I knew you were in pain? I know you, Freddy. I've lived with you. I've loved you. Love you. Your pain was my pain and I wanted to ease it, but you pushed me away."

"Guilt, Margo," Freddy admitted. "Powerful guilt."

"I know, Freddy. I have eyes. Feelings. Intuition. I could see that. But that still shouldn't make you push me away."

"The guilt doesn't go away that easily," Freddy said. "Pain like that doesn't stop overnight."

"But you feared something like this happening, after all."

"Yes, for a long time, but did I do my best to stop it? Did I try everything to help Gabrielle, my wife? I saw trouble early on, sure. It took a toll on me. I'm sure on us. Should I have done something else?"

"You did your best, Freddy. I know you. Stop torturing yourself. I can't stand to see you suffer like this. Not fair to you. Not fair to Marguerite."

In Paris, the authorities ruled Gabrielle's death accidental. They didn't have to tell Freddy that, because he already knew.

"I spoke with Gabrielle early in the morning that day, and the night before, too," Freddy confessed to Margo. "We were going to talk more at home in London. Gabrielle wanted to try working things out between us. I didn't tell you that, Margo, and I'm sorry."

"It wasn't necessary."

"But you had the right to know."

"So I did," Margo said, "but it doesn't matter now." She paused and again Freddy envisioned her rubbing her elbow. "Would you have done it? I mean gone back to Gabrielle?"

Freddy thought about that in the hours after the phone conversation with Gabrielle. How long she would embrace her new life was open to speculation. Would she keep her word? Who knew what she would do? He certainly didn't. Freddy felt guilty for thinking so at the time, but he was burnt enough times buying Gabrielle's promises.

"I would go back only for the sake of our child," Freddy said. "Marguerite needed both parents."

"Yes, I believe that, Freddy. I know you. The goodness in you would do nothing else."

"Gabrielle was a loving mother," Freddy said, "but toward the end she was running away from Marguerite, too. I felt that. The Paris apartment became her sanctuary and at the same time her hell."

"So sad," Margo said. "I'm sorry for Gabrielle, I really am." After a long pause, she added, "Freddy?"

"What?"

"I can't help thinking . . . wondering . . ." Margo hesitated. "Freddy, and what about your life? What would've happened to you if you went back to Gabrielle? Would you've been happy? Would you've loved her like before? Would you still be Freddy?

All fair questions that Freddy mulled over before Gabrielle's death. He still did. Still no answers.

34

The ceremony was small and elegant, held in the garden at George Paulik's estate in Lake Forest. Freddy was best man and Marguerite flower girl. Phil confessed to being happy just eloping, but Sheila thought it unfair to make her throw away the silver spoon altogether.

Later, leaning against a big oak tree, Freddy watched Marguerite and Kristen sashay around like a pair of debutantes. Kristen was slowly warming up to him, as well as becoming a big sister to Marguerite. Since flying back to Chicago from Los Angeles after the cross-country drive, Freddy encouraged Marguerite to spend time with Kristen. The two were inseparable now and he liked seeing that.

Freddy lit a cigar and watched Phil and Sheila dance. They were laughing. They looked happy. He remembered writing Rufus and Effie how happy he was to be marrying Gabrielle. By then Margo was married to Howard and already had Kristen.

"Is this what you really want?" Rufus wrote. "Don't look for Margo in this one."

Not that Freddy considered Gabrielle as a second choice to Margo. Anything but. Gabrielle was too stunning with too much presence to be number two to anybody, including Margo. "Margo and I were something special, but Margo's gone," Freddy wrote back. "Maybe I can create another special *something* with Gabrielle."

The wedding glittered. Freddy wanted something small and intimate, but Gabrielle complained that they were not peasants. In the end, Prince Hamid gave the bride away at his opulent chateau outside Paris. Years later, the prince also helped Freddy convince Gabrielle to enter the rehabilitation clinic in Switzerland. She was okay for a time, but soon the old Gabrielle returned.

At the funeral, Prince Hamid put a hand on Freddy's shoulder and said no one could save Gabrielle. Freddy confessed to not trying hard enough. Hamid assured him he did all he could. "Perhaps in the end," Hamid believed, "God had other plans for that beautiful woman."

"Tell that to Marguerite, my friend," Freddy said to Prince Hamid back then.

Freddy re-lit his cigar and focused on Chicago Trio, a student ensemble from the conservatory, that sweetened the late August sunshine with a stream of charming salon music. The kids reminded Freddy of Kreutzer Trio in the beginning. He arranged the salon pieces Kreutzer Trio played and later donated the music to the conservatory library, the same music Chicago Trio was now playing at the wedding.

From the other side of the garden, Margo turned and smiled at Freddy, a smile of remembrance, he thought. He returned the smile. Her smile widened and she put a hand on her heart as a sign of taking his love. Then as Freddy watched her walk toward him, he remembered a comment he made to her long ago: "It will always be like this for us — love forever."

Now he had to question the sincerity of his comment all those years ago. If it was still love forever, why did he feel so uneasy to be around Margo?

"You looked like you were so far away," she said, rubbing his arm. "Anything you want to share?"

Freddy shook his head no. "Just thinking," he said.

She pulled away with a look of concern and said nothing.

"The kids sound good, don't they," Freddy said, nodding toward the trio.

"Very good," Margo agreed, "but not as good as we did at that age." She rubbed her elbow. "I don't hear the same fire in their soul, the same passion in their playing. Not the same romance. I don't, Freddy."

"The same tyrant pushing them," Freddy laughed, remembering

Margo barking at him for being a tyrant.

"Somebody needed to push us," she admitted. "Without you, we'd still be talking about forming the trio and then going out for coffee."

"Without you and Phil it wasn't possible," Freddy reminded her. "You, both of you, had the sound I wanted, and the heart to go along with it."

The waiter brought Freddy another Jack Daniels.

Margo took Freddy's arm again. "How many have you had?"

Freddy took a drink. "I've lost count."

"Don't you think you should slow down?" Margo gently scolded him. "You still have Marguerite to take care of."

Freddy nodded. "I can't go around chasing my own tail anymore, you mean."

Margo regarded him again. "Are you sure you're okay? You look a little . . ." her voice trailed off.

Freddy nodded again, knowing that without Marguerite to hold on to, he would collapse like a tower.

"What can I do, Freddy? You know you're not alone in this."

"This one I have to work out for myself," he said.

"And what happens to us, then?"

"God, I wish I knew. I'm putting one foot in front of the other, destination lost in fog."

"Well, Freddy, you keep walking," Margo said, dejected, and then turned and walked away without a word.

Freddy didn't try to stop her.

35

Freddy thought the Eric Satie anecdote fit him perfectly: that people kept telling the French composer to wait till he was 50 and he would see and Satie said he was 50 and he still didn't see anything. With the way his life was going at 40 Freddy wasn't sure he'd see anything even at 70.

In the days after the wedding, the only things that made sense to Freddy was to be with Marguerite. He didn't see Margo, and when he called her, the conversation was lifeless. Phil and Sheila were on their honeymoon. Most of the time Freddy floated around Chicago with Marguerite. Father and daughter on an expedition, he announced every day before leaving the hotel. They visited museums. Went to concerts, movies and they walked along Lake Michigan. Freddy often talked about a Cubs game at Wrigley Field as being a memorable experience. After he took Marguerite to a game, she wouldn't stop talking about it. And to cap the Chicago experience, they feasted on deep dish pizza and Chicago style hotdogs.

George Paulik took them on his yacht to Door County in Wisconsin for fish boil, one of the great wonders of the world, Freddy promised Marguerite. Throughout the trip, Paulik kept mum on the subject of getting Freddy on the conservatory's faculty, and eventually moving back to Chicago. Freddy knew the old fox had not forgotten anything and that he was waiting for the right moment to pop the question.

Marguerite spent one night with Rufus and Effie. The next day Freddy and Effie rehearsed some of the tunes they planned for the tribute recording to Connie and Luke. On "Early Autumn," Marguerite became teary eyed. Sitting on the piano bench with Freddy, she said, "Daddy, did grandmother sing that, too?"

"Woody Herman's tune," Freddy said. "Yes, my darling, she sang it many times."

"It's so lovely, Daddy."

"Delicious, sugar, just like you."

"Did grandmother also sing it to grandfather?"

"Oh honey," Effie chimed in, "that girl, Connie, your grandmother, she would lean against the piano and look into your grandfather's eyes and, oh-my-dear-my-darlin', you could see sparks fly like it was the Fourth of July. And your grandfather, handsome like a prince, he'd sweep across the keyboard like a bird in the sky. Oh, that was so sweet, honey girl."

"And he blew your grandmother a kiss and you saw her face light up like a rose," Freddy added, now misty eyed. "Then your grand-mother placed a hand on her heart, as though pledging allegiance, and closed her eyes. It was her way of saying she loved him complete-ly. I was a little boy, sugar, about your age, and how well I remember all that."

"They must have loved each other very much, Daddy," Marguerite said, allowing her father to wipe her tears, and then turning to Effie, added, "Don't you think so, aunt Effie?"

Effie, her eyes filled with love, nodded yes.

"When I fall in love and marry, I want the same," Marguerite said. "Will I have that, Aunt Effie?"

"Oh honey, with that beautiful face and the lovely heart to match, you'll have the world lining up to take your hand."

"And you'll promenade on a gilded carpet like a queen," Freddy followed, already seeing his daughter radiating with her mother's beauty.

In the car on the way to the hotel, Marguerite was quiet. It was early afternoon. Freddy brushed a hand on her cheek. "A kiss for your thoughts, sugar," he said.

"I was thinking . . ." Marguerite paused. "Daddy, I want to know more about Luke and Connie. I mean my grandfather and grandmother." She studied her father's profile. "Was grandmother very beautiful, like Mummy?"

Luke always introduced Connie as the "beautiful Connie Lacourt," Freddy recalled. They never made an entrance on the stage together. Luke wanted Connie's to be with majesty, under the spotlight, as if nothing else existed on the stage. Luke first played a few tunes and then introduced her, and Connie swept onto the stage like an empress and took the microphone, which was placed for her on the piano.

Then there were the times when Connie worked in her little garden, Freddy remembered, and they heard strains of Luke's piano drifting through the French doors like perfumed air. Sometimes Connie hummed along with the music and sometimes sang along softly, her face bright and beautiful like the flowers in her garden she loved so much.

Years later in London, sometimes while Freddy played the big grand in his study, he heard Gabrielle say from the garden, "Freddy, *cheri*, how lovely your music." Freddy loved those musical moments like the ones in the little garden in New Orleans.

From the passenger seat, Marguerite tugged at Freddy's sleeve, breaking his thoughts.

"Yes, my darling, your grandmother was beautiful, like Mummy," he said. "Your grandmother had French blood, too, like Mummy. She was born in New Orleans, but her parents came from France."

"And grandfather?"

"Also born and raised in New Orleans, but his parents came from the north of England."

"So that makes me . . ."

"British, French and American, because I was born in New Orleans. Splendid mixture, what?" Freddy said.

"Oh Daddy, what a silly boy you are," Marguerite chuckled at his fake British accent.

"Now, how about that kiss you promised me for my thoughts, my good man?" Marguerite puckered her lips and closed her eyes.

Freddy touched a finger on his lips and then on hers. "A kiss for my beautiful queen," he said.

36

Freddy avoided Margo for several days. He just couldn't bear to be near her, or even talk to her on the phone. He tried, but he couldn't make himself. He still loved Margo, but only from behind a barrier, like a bittersweet fruit that he didn't want to touch. Marguerite was the one who drove him to telephone Margo Friday morning, the weekend before their planned return to London in time for school.

"Daddy, don't you like Margo anymore?" she asked at breakfast in the hotel restaurant.

The question came out of nowhere and surprised Freddy. "Why do you say that, sugar?"

Marguerite shrugged. "I don't know. Because."

In the early morning light Marguerite's resemblance to Gabrielle was remarkable. Freddy imagined how Gabrielle must have looked at Marguerite's age. "Because of what, sweetheart?"

Marguerite shrugged again. "I like Margo very much and miss her. She's my favorite next to Mummy."

After breakfast Freddy telephoned Margo at home. Josh said to try her mobile. Margo was on the train heading downtown. She answered. "I thought you'd already escaped to London."

Her voice was iced and Freddy felt the chill. "You're mad at me."

"How does pissed off sound?"

"Not what I expected from a genteel . . ."

"What did you expect, Freddy?" Margo cut him off. "For days not a word from you, nothing."

Freddy always loved Margo's even temper, especially during the rough times, when she had a way of smoothing everything around her. This Margo, however, was borderline Gabrielle in her anger, he thought.

"Sorry, kiddo, I should have called."

"So then what do I owe the honor to?"

"Well, how would you like to have lunch with Marguerite and me?"

Margo was quiet for moment before saying, "Love to have lunch with Marguerite, but as for you, you can piss off in your stupid red Camaro, mister whatever's-going-on-in-your-head."

Freddy was the last to admit he knew what was going on in his head. He tried to make light of the atmosphere. "Margo, my love, please mind your Catholic upbringing."

"Oh, shut up, Freddy," she snapped. "Meet me at the shop. Goodbye."

Freddy thought he heard her mobile phone fly clear across the train car.

On the walk from the hotel to Margo's shop later in the morning, Freddy and Marguerite stopped in a music store for the latest release by a rock group Freddy never heard of. He raised an eyebrow at the near nude female pictured on the CD cover. "You sure this girl's a singer and not a stripper?" he said.

"What's a stripper, Daddy?"

"Well . . ." he didn't know how to answer that. "What happened to the girl's clothes?"

"Oh Daddy, you're being so silly." Marguerite rolled her eyes. "Don't you know she looks cool?"

"That so?"

"But of course, my good man."

"My apologies, oh queen of the Nile."

"Poor dear, how little you know about us women," Marguerite chuckled shaking her head.

"You have no idea how little, my butterfly." Freddy wrapped an arm around her shoulder. "I'm like the guy who, when he hears a blond soprano singing in the bath tub, puts his ear to the keyhole. Heard that one somewhere."

"You're impossible, Daddy," Marguerite said, and trying to stretch her little arm around him, she added, "but I love you anyway, all of Bruch's Scottish Fantasy."

"And I love you all of Brahms' first piano concerto. How about that, sugar?"

"And you love Brahms so much, Daddy. Wonderful."

They drifted to the classical section. All of Freddy's recordings were in the bins. "Trout Quintet" snapped him back to Steyer, Austria, where he recorded the music, and he lost himself in the memory of the time spent there with Gabrielle and Marguerite. A while later he felt Marguerite tugging at his sleeve and saying, "Are you all right, Daddy? You look a little weird."

"Yes, my darling, I'm fine." Freddy drew her close to him. "With you near me, I'm always fine and dandy."

Marguerite's eyes filled with dew when she noticed the "Trout Quintet" recording. "We miss Mummy a lot, don't we, Daddy?"

"Yes, sugar, we do." He put the CD back in the bin and then led Marguerite away.

"Do you think Mummy is very happy now, Daddy? Finally, I mean."

"Why do you say that, sugar — 'Finally.'"

"Because."

"Don't you think Mummy was happy when we had her? Did she ever tell you so?"

Marguerite wiped her tears and shook her head no. "I just knew Mummy was sad sometimes."

"I'm sorry, baby, why didn't you ever tell me?"

Marguerite shrugged.

Freddy stopped and knelt before her. "Do you feel like telling me now?"

Marguerite shook her head no.

"Maybe someday you'll tell me, then?"

She nodded yes.

Freddy kissed her nose and wiped her tears. "Your Mummy loved you very much."

Marguerite nodded yes.

"And Mummy will always love you and watch over you, you know that, don't you?" Freddy added.

In *Swan*, Marguerite ran up to Margo and melted in her embrace. Margo threw a quizzical look at Freddy and he signaled that they would talk about it later. After lunch, Margo took Marguerite shopping and then on the train to her house for a sleepover. Freddy returned to the hotel and telephoned Bob Chase in London to go over his schedule for the upcoming season.

He had concerts in Paris, Vienna, Prague, Amsterdam, Berlin, Munich, London and Buenos Aires. In America, he was scheduled in New York, Washington D.C., Philadelphia and Atlanta. Later in Chicago. In three weeks, Rufus and Effie were flying to London to make the tribute recording. Later in the year, Freddy also Planned to record the complete Debussy and Ravel, and the complete "Iberia" by Isaac Albeniz.

When he finished with Bob Chase, Freddy packed a bag for the weekend for Marguerite — her pillow, and her teddy bear Mr. Mendelssohn. He drove to Margo's in his rented red Camaro. They ordered pizza for dinner. Afterwards Josh went to a friend's house. Kristen took Marguerite upstairs to her bedroom to watch TV.

Freddy slid behind the piano keyboard for a Chopin nocturn. Margo brought him a Jack Daniels and then sank in the couch with a glass of port.

"Still angry with me?" Freddy said over the music.

"Pissed off, you mean," Margo said. "A little."

"A little pissed off doesn't sound as bad as a lot of angry." Freddy stopped playing and drank his whiskey.

"I reserve angry for special occasions," Margo said, without looking at Freddy, "and we've had a few between us, in case you've forgotten. Or maybe you need a reminder. Let me see, where shall I start?"

"I haven' forgotten a thing," Freddy ignored the sniping, and returned his attention to Chopin. He loved Chopin. It went back to the days when Luke played Chopin. Luke knew the nocturns, and the ballades, too. He always said that Chopin was the one pianist he would love to have been. For him, Luke said, Chopin was everything, from romantic to soulful to heroic and tragic. There was no one with Chopin's piano soul, Luke said.

"Where are you, Freddy?" Margo said.

"I don't know where I am. Sometimes I think in Hades with Orpheus."

"That's reassuring."

"Yeah, well." He stopped playing. "The only thing that keeps my head screwed on is Marguerite."

"She's precious."

"Yes, she is, thank you. I lost my parents, and she lost her mother, but that little girl isn't going to lose her father. Not a chance."

Margo refreshed her port, and Freddy's whiskey. "And what about the big girl down here?" she asked. "Where does she fit in this place of yours, wherever it is."

Freddy started to play again, but stopped and drank his whiskey.

"Please tell me, Freddy," Margo went on. "I feel I've become an imposition."

"You're not."

"So you say," Margo snapped. "I come home after the funeral and for weeks hardly hear a word from you. Then you breeze through town in that stupid red Camaro and then you're gone cross country."

"What do you have against the Camaro?"

"Because it's your red whore and I'm sick and tired of seeing it. That's a good name for it — Red Whore. Now every red car that I see reminds me of it."

Suddenly Margo was beyond pissed off. She was angry. Freddy saw almost the same anger toward the end in London and sometimes it forced him to escape their little flat and lose himself on the streets. He wanted to do it now: to get in the Camaro, his Red Whore, and burn rubber to who knew where, anywhere, as long as it was away from Margo.

"For weeks I hear nothing from you," Margo continued, still angry, "and then at the wedding you avoid me like I have a disease, or I'm some repulsive creature. Shall I continue?"

Freddy slammed the piano lid shut. "What do you want from me, Margo? What, damn it?"

"I don't know," she shouted, and then quietly, "I don't know, Freddy. Maybe . . . Maybe I want my old Freddy back."

"The old Freddy is dead. Life killed him."

"Don't say that," Margo said, her even temper returning to calm things down. "Oh God, Freddy, just the thought of losing you destroys me. Please, Freddy, I don't want to hear that kind of talk. It's horrible."

Freddy pushed away from the piano and stood looking out the window. The Camaro was parked out front. Margo came over and put a hand on his arm.

"I wake up in the middle of the night, sweating, and I want to scream," Freddy began after a while, still gazing out the window, "and I see Gabrielle dying. She's trying to reach the phone to call me. I want to believe that. And where am I? In Chicago, that's where I am. Gabrielle's lying on the floor in the damn Paris apartment, her sanctuary, all alone, playing her final role, her death scene over again, like in *Algerian Dawn,* and here I am breathing heavy with my girlfriend." He stopped and squeezed his temples.

Margo buried her face in her hands. "You make everything sound so ugly and so dirty." Tears broke her voice.

"Maybe inside I am both of those things," Freddy said," "as well as cruel and selfish and uncaring and angry and every other dark thing you can imagine."

He watched Margo run out of the room in tears. He wanted to go after her, to put his arms around her. He realized he hurt her, as he did Gabrielle. Damn, life was really beating him to death.

Freddy was still at the window when Margo returned, her hair tied in a ponytail and her make up off. Suddenly he was looking at the same beautiful face he saw for the first time at that party so long ago.

Margo walked over to the window and again put a hand on his arm. "I wonder how long this new nightmare will haunt you?" she said in a soft voice. "How long will Gabrielle's nightmare rattle your insides? God knows, you already have a gallery of them — things that haunt you."

Freddy shook his head and turned back to the Camaro.

"The Camaro is the past, Freddy," Margo reminded him. "Let it go. Let sweet Aurore rest in peace. And Kreutzer Trio, too. And the old days. It's not the Chicago we had together. Maybe my old Freddy, the love of my life, is gone, you're right, but I will not give up on this Freddy, the one in my house, in my life."

Freddy wrapped her in his arms. He kissed her. They had not been this close since making love in his hotel room. Margo felt good in his arms. Her kiss was sweet.

"Your parents are gone," Margo murmured, then. "Gabrielle is gone. In time I hope you keep a proper distance from them. Let them go, Freddy."

"It's not that easy, Margo."

"I know, darling," Margo said, and kissed his cheek. "Look around you, Freddy. This is now. Come back to it. This is your reality. It's all here for you. Sure, this home has its own ghosts, my God, but they know their place. They don't rule here. This is your home, too, and Marguerite's."

"I had a home a long time ago with Connie and Luke," Freddy said, "and nothing else seems to fit."

"And what about that little girl — Marguerite? Doesn't she need a home and family?"

"Of course, she does."

"Then make this her home, Freddy. Let her live here while you're chasing your ghosts. She loves it here. The kids love her. I love her. She'll be around family."

Freddy looked into Margo's eyes. "And where do I leave myself?" he said.

37

After Freddy took Marguerite back to London for school, he encouraged her to telephone Margo, Kristen and Effie whenever she wanted. He also encouraged her to write them letters. Yet his own letters and phone calls slowed to a trickle, especially to Margo.

A month later, he flew Rufus and Effie to London for the tribute recording. The CD was a smash hit. There was a flurry of radio, television and newspaper interviews. Freddy took many of them, and Effie as many as she could physically handle. Rufus said Effie was flying high with her sudden fame. Phil wrote a big article on the life of Connie and Luke.

"Listening to Effie and you in your musical tribute to Luke and Connie," Sheila wrote, "I realize what you mean about their magical sound. So intimate. And Effie's voice and your piano — so intoxicating."

George Paulik called to congratulate Freddy on the recording. Not a word about the move to Chicago, but Freddy knew the old fox had forgotten nothing.

Margo telephoned and said the music's sultry mood made her feel like sitting down with a cigarette and a bottle of Jack Daniels.

"Since when do you smoke cigarettes and drink bourbon?" Freddy said.

"I'm thinking of starting," Margo said.

"What, is this the new you?"

"You know me, I'm hot to trot."

"Jesus, Margo, your parents will never forgive me for corrupting you."

"My parents will forgive you anything." She laughed. "God knows what they see in you."

"Must be my southern charm."

"Must be something, *Frederick*," she said, impersonating her mother, who always called him by his full first name. "My parents liked Howard," Margo went on. "I mean who couldn't help but like him. Howard was sweet and caring, but he wasn't *Frederick*. No one was."

They talked about a lot of other things, except what they really wanted to talk about, Freddy thought. He could hear the strain in Margo's voice, but it was nowhere near what he heard in his. He felt awkward talking to Margo. When making plans for the anniversary celebration the year before, he couldn't wait to see her. Now just the thought of being in the same room with Margo slapped him with Gabrielle's death scene.

Then suddenly Margo said, "I saw your picture in People magazine with that actress, Stephanie Carnes."

The suddenness of her comment took him by surprise. He never told her about Stephanie, or any other woman he knew, for that matter. He didn't know why.

"Kristen showed me the photo of the two of you together," Margo explained, "and I don't think she was all that pleased. I think she was starting to come around the idea that you and I were an item and not you and the actress, but I set her straight."

Freddy knew which photo Margo meant. It was taken at a bistro following his performance with the New York Philharmonic. Stephanie Carnes was an actress Freddy knew for many years. Stephanie drowned in a difficult marriage and her career was stalled.

"It's just a picture, Margo, and we're just friends and nothing else," Freddy assured her.

"You looked so cozy together, Freddy, so touchy-feely," Margo was not listening. "She's very beautiful, you know, but then you always had an eye for beautiful women."

"Yes, I did. Look at you."

"I wasn't fishing for a compliment."

"We're two of a kind, Stephanie and I, both carrying heavy bag-gage and looking for someplace to put it down for a while."

"Oh, goodness gracious, I'm so glad you told me that," Margo an-nounced, sarcasm wrapped around every word. "Now I can sleep in peace knowing the truth."

"It's not what you think, Margo."

"I don't think anymore." She stopped and thought. "No, I don't care to think anything from here on."

"We're not sleeping together, if you care to listen," Freddy tried to defend himself. "I'm not sleeping with anybody. What more can I say?"

"Now that's reassuring. So grownup."

"Damn it, Margo, if you're not going to listen, what more do you want from me? What do you people, all of you, what do you want from me?"

"I'm not just any people, Freddy, or have you forgotten?" Margo paused a moment and Freddy could visualize her rubbing her elbow. "Oh, what's the use?" she said, then. "This conversation isn't even worth my time. Goodbye, Freddy. Send Marguerite over next time she has a long holiday from school. We all miss her." She paused again. "As for you, mister whoever-you-are-these-days, you do what you want, and chase all the women you want, and sleep around all you want, and then look your daughter in the eye. Look me in the eye. Shame on you, Freddy." She hung up.

He was angry with her for not listening to him, and angry with himself for giving Margo the impression that he was chasing women.

"Did you know what the hell you were doing?" Phil asked him on the phone from Chicago. "How did you expect Margo to feel seeing your pictures?"

"Nothing is going on with any of the women, Phil," Freddy ex-plained. "I just got tired of eating dinner alone."

"Tell that to Margo."

"I did, but she wasn't listening. I've never seen her so angry."

"Boy, you sure know how to piss off the people who love you."

"Yes, well, I have a special talent for that."

"So then how long does all this go on?" Phil wondered.

"Till the twittering in my head stops."

"Or Margo calls it quits on you for good," Phil warned. "Thought about that?"

"Losing Margo would be like losing a big part of myself," Freddy said. "Still, every time I get close to her, guilt tears me up. I see Gabrielle."

As he expected, Margo did not call him again, and the twittering in his head kept on. Then one afternoon Marguerite surprised him when she wrapped her little arms around his neck and said, "Are you very unhappy, Daddy?"

He was in his study listening to Effie's voice on the sound system.

"Why do you ask, Sugar?" He pulled Marguerite onto his lap.

"Because," she said, and buried her face in the small of his neck.

"Because of what? You think you can tell me?"

"You won't die like Mummy, will you, Daddy? Mummy was not very happy. Is that why she died?"

Once before Marguerite mentioned about her mother being un-happy, but she did not want to talk about it.

"No, sugar, I won't die," Freddy reassured her. "I'll be here forever to love you." He kissed her brow.

"Oh good," Marguerite said. "I was worried, Daddy."

"But how do you know Mummy was not very happy?" Freddy quizzed her.

"Because she said so," Marguerite whimpered. "I overheard her on the telephone speaking with Prince Hamid."

Later that day, Freddy telephoned Prince Hamid, who was on business in Saudi Arabia.

"I spoke with Gabrielle many times," Prince Hamid said, "and again just before . . ."

"Did I make her that unhappy, Hamid?" Freddy said, feeling a des-perate need to know.

"No one would have made that troubled girl happy," the prince believed. "And she knew you did not love her enough. I tried to rea-son with her more than once, but she knew your Margo was your only love." Prince Hamid paused, then. "Sadly, my friend, Gabrielle said she had never loved you completely either."

"The tragedy of our marriage," Freddy said, feeling defeated. "I think I knew how she felt. You see, my dear friend, I have seen true love first hand — my parents. But no, I saw no sign of true happiness in my own marriage."

"Know this, Freddy," Prince Hamid said. "I believe Gabrielle was not capable of loving anybody completely. She did not have the mechanism. She could no more give herself to you than she could to others."

"How ironic, then," Freddy said, "that before she died, Gabrielle wanted to give us another chance. She called me in Chicago."

"Perhaps her love for you was deserving of another chance," Hamid said. "Perhaps she did love you more than you think. Who knows about such things?"

"We will never find out, will we?"

"Sometimes it's the way of life."

"At least I want to believe that in the end Gabrielle did try for us," Freddy said. "I'm going to have to hold on to that for my own peace of mind."

38

Long ago, Luke told Freddy to never take audience adulation for granted, and to enjoy the applause with grace and humility, thanking his lucky stars that he wasn't getting a kick in the ass instead.

Years later, in the Kreutzer Trio days, whenever Margo complained about shaking too many hands and smiling, Freddy reminded her of something else Luke said: "Never let a fan walk away disappointed in meeting you."

On the flight to Chicago, Freddy wished he never heard his father's advice, not if he had to listen to the barrage of chatter from the seats across. Any other time, yes, and thank you, but not now, not today. He wanted Rufus on his mind and nothing else.

The couple sitting across the aisle was dazzled by Freddy's performance of the of Beethoven "Emperor" Piano Concerto in Atlanta the previous evening. They had all of his recordings and they especially loved the charming tribute recording to his parents: *Silk and Honey*. That one of the reigning concert pianists in the world was also an American — "with a name you can actually pronounce" — was even a bigger honor in their eyes, they said.

Freddy smiled and thanked them for the umpteenth time before they finally left him alone to close his eyes for a few minutes and focus his thoughts on Rufus. He remembered the day he auditioned for Rufus, who was the director of jazz studies, a new department at Chicago Conservatory of Music.

"You're Luke and Connie's boy?" Freddy remembered Rufus saying. Then Rufus nodded at the piano and added, "Now let's see what you can do, boy."

Freddy did. Playing from memory, he spent a half hour on his musical journey that spanned a range of musical styles and periods. Rufus was dazzled.

Years earlier, Luke told Freddy what Schubert's teacher Wenzel Ruzicka, from the Imperial Royal Seminary in Vienna, said about the young composer: that he learned it all from God. "That's you, my little Freddy," Luke said, squeezing his son in his arms. "Someday you'll be on the concert stage and make your mother and me proud."

So long ago.

From across the aisle on the airplane, Freddy heard, "Are you playing in Chicago this week, Mister Priestley?"

Freddy's mind took a while to digest the question. "No, no," he answered, "Philadelphia next week. I'm seeing some friends in Chicago."

They said they heard him play the Rachmaninoff Third in Chicago during the conservatory's celebration a year ago and found the music and his playing reaching into their soul. Freddy nodded his thanks, half way listening to the conversation, his mind drifting back to Margo's telephone call earlier that morning. It was right after Freddy returned from jogging and was packing for his flight to Philadelphia that evening.

It was not the news Freddy wanted to hear from Margo, because Rufus was a god and gods did not suffer heart attacks. He rerouted his flight with a stopover in Chicago for a few days. When he walked into the hospital in Chicago, luggage in hand, he saw everyone gathered in the waiting room and felt almost paralyzed. Effie rushed into his arms and burst into tears, and didn't let go until Freddy managed to calm her down. Hugs from Phil, Sheila and Paulik followed. Then Margo.

"Hello stranger," she said.

"Hello yourself, gorgeous." Freddy wrapped her in his arms. "I wasn't sure what kind of reception I'd get from you."

"I wasn't sure either." Margo brushed a loving hand on his temple.

"Does this mean I'm forgiven?"

"I don't know about that," Margo said, easing out of his embrace.

"You've lost a lot of weight. Don't you eat anymore?"

"I eat . . . sometimes."

"That's not very smart."

"I know. I seem to have lost my appetite for a lot of things."

A nurse led Freddy to see Rufus and gave him five minutes. Freddy sat on the edge of bed and held Rufus' hand. "Now see what you've done to yourself," he said. "All that sinful jazz music, that's what it is."

Rufus gave Freddy's hand a gentle squeeze. "How are you, boy?" His voice was weak and straining. "I knew you wouldn't let old Rufus die without seeing his son."

"You're not dying, Ruf," Freddy said, fighting back his tears. No sir, not this time around, Freddy told himself. He lost enough: his parents, Gabrielle. He was not going to lose Rufus, too. Out of the question.

"I'll be goddamned if I'm going to let you go," Freddy said.

"Rufus tried a smile. "Better not let Effie hear you blaspheme. She . . ."

"Don't you speak the Lord's name in vain, young man," Freddy growled, impersonating Effie. "Now you ask for the Lord's forgiveness, hear? Go on."

Rufus tried to smile again. "Listen, boy."

"Don't talk, Ruf. Just lie down and daydream."

"Important, boy." Rufus struggled with his breath. "I want you to take care of our Effie. If I don't make it through, you take care of her."

"Of course, I will, Ruf. She's my family. My mother. I'll always take care of her."

"Good boy. I know you will."

"I'll take care of both of you," Freddy said, his hands smothering Ruf's. "But you're not going anywhere. Ease up on the club. On the conservatory. Stay home and grow a garden. Write a book on jazz. Write your memoire, better yet." Freddy thought a moment and added, "Margo and I will take care of you both."

"Ah, Missy, a beautiful girl." Ruf's voice was growing weaker. "Mourn Gabrielle. Mourn your wife. That poor girl wasn't lucky like the rest of us. God had his reason for taking her. Just like he took your mama and daddy." Rufus stopped, struggling with his breath. "When you're done mourning, soon I hope, then you take Missy's hand and make a life for yourselves."

"I will, Ruf. I promise."

"Let her go once . . . you did. God's given you another chance. More than a lot of other people get." Rufus paused again and closed his eyes. "Do it for Connie and Luke, for little Marguerite, for Kristen and Josh, Margo's children. Do it for our family, boy. Do that for those who love you, for old Rufus and Effie. For all of us." Rufus then drifted to sleep.

For the next few days, Freddy spent much of his time with Effie and Rufus. He slept at Effie's. He drove her to the hospital in the morning and stayed until Effie sent him out, saying he shouldn't be cooped up with old and sick people. Margo stopped in every day. Freddy took her to lunch. She said nothing about Stephanie Carnes, or the other women Freddy was seen with.

Freddy flew to Philadelphia late in the week for his concert Saturday evening, and was back in Chicago Sunday. By then Rufus was well enough to sit up in bed and make eyes at all the nurses, according to Effie. The day before leaving for London, Freddy took Rufus home.

"So much has happened since we were here last," Margo reminded Freddy that evening at the little Italian restaurant where they ate lunch many times. "Seems like the world's been turned inside out."

Freddy reached across the table to take her hands, but Margo pulled back. "Please don't, Freddy," she begged.

"Now what did I do to piss you off?" Freddy said.

Margo studied him. "Just tell me this, what really made you push me away this past year?"

Freddy made a face and threw up his hands. "Guilt, Margo. Painful guilt. I've told you. Sliced me wide open and ripped out my insides."

"So you take it out all on me," Margo snapped. "What did I do except to love you? Try to comfort you. Help you get over your pain."

"Suddenly I couldn't stand being near you. Touching you." Freddy stopped and shook his head in disbelief. "My God, what am I saying? I've loved you most of my life. Love you with all my heart. Without you I have no life. But there it is. I couldn't help the guilt."

Margo's eyes turned cold. "How reassuring for me to hear all this."

"I've never lied to you," Freddy said. "It's the way I felt. Sometimes still feel. Hurts me to say it."

Freddy reached for her hands again and this time Margo did not flinch. Except that her hands were cold and lifeless. Unresponsive. Freddy let go and sank back in his seat.

"So then every time I thought of you I saw Gabrielle pointing a finger at me, and screaming. Guilt, Margo. I don't know what else to say?"

"And then here I am. How can you stand it?"

"By loving you more than ever, if that's possible," Freddy confessed.

"Until when, Freddy?" Margo dabbed her eyes with her napkin. "Until another guilt attack?"

"I love you, Margo."

"And I love you, Freddy, she said, wiping her tears, "but you come with a heavy price tag, I'm finally realizing. You hurt too much and I can't take the pain anymore." She picked up her purse and rose.

"Margo, please, don't do this."

"I think I want to go home now," she announced. "It's my turn to get away from you."

Freddy paid the check and followed her out.

"Don't do this to me again," he repeated. "Don't walk away. Not another Heathrow."

"I must to survive you, Freddy. Goodbye."

Her tone was calm, but Freddy felt the numbing chill in it. "Margo, please, I need you. Don't walk away." Freddy doubted, though, that Margo heard him.

She hailed a taxi. "You know something else, Freddy," she said, opening the taxi door. "I've had enough of riding in a Camaro for one lifetime."

Freddy watched the taxi drive off. No Camaro for him this time around. He would walk.

39

Rufus passed away in his sleep on a warm spring night. He was 81.

Effie told Margo that she always believed the Lord put her man on earth and gave him beautiful music to feed the earth like sweet rain, and when Rufus was done with his work, he was called to heaven to play his music for eternity.

Margo reached Freddy in Buenos Aires with the news. That evening Freddy was to perform the Schumann A-Minor Piano Concerto, one of Margo's favorites. He had not seen Margo for months, and only spoken with her a handful of times over the phone. "Seems lately I'm bearer of bad news for you, Freddy," Margo said, and burst into tears. Freddy listened with a broken heart.

"Rufus gave me a good talking a few days ago," Margo said after a while. "He was feeling good, except for complaining Effie wouldn't let him smoke his cigars." Margo paused, still crying. "Freddy, this has gone long enough. Come home, my darling."

"Yes, home," Freddy said, realizing how right Margo was. She was the love of his life and his home was where she was. Ruf's passing suddenly slapped him with that reality. Enough was enough, Margo was always right.

"Rufus wanted you here with me. With the family," Margo said.

"I know, sugar, I know. I realize that now. My home's always been with you." Then he could not hold back his tears.

"Oh, Freddy, don't," Margo begged, crying along with him. She saw him cry only once, long ago, when he told her about the death of his parents. She felt his pain then, and she felt it now. "Don't, Freddy. Ruf wouldn't want you . . ." Her voice trailed off as her tears welled up.

After a while Freddy said, "I wonder if that beautiful man knew how much I loved him."

"He knew, Freddy. You were the son he never had. He told me often. And he was so proud of you, Freddy. You could see it in his eyes every time your name came up."

Freddy thought about his concert that evening and wondered if he was up to performing. He felt drained, his fingers and heart disconnected. He squeezed his temples. "Without Rufus I don't know where I would be."

"You'd still be way up there, my darling. I know you. And you forget, you also had Luke and Connie."

"Yes, I did have them all."

"Most of all, you've had Frederick Priestley himself in your corner," she reminded him.

"And my beautiful Margo."

"You've always had me in your corner, my darling, even when you were gone from me for so long."

"Even after being a womanizer?"

"You still have some explaining to do about that, mister," Margo said. Her tone betrayed forgiveness. "I should slap your face, but now's not the time."

"Nothing happened with any of them, Margo. We're just friends. You've got to believe me."

"I do, Freddy. I know you. I have to be angry at something." She was silent for a time. "Freddy," she said, then, "are you up to playing tonight?"

Freddy considered her question. "People expect a concert from Frederick Priestley and, by God, they'll have one. Otherwise Ruf will skin me alive." Then imitating Ruf's raspy tone, Freddy growled, "Don't you turn chicken shit on me, boy. You get your ass out there and show them what Frederick Priestley can do."

Both were silent before bursting out laughing. "God, Ruf would never forgive me if I let things get in the way of my playing," Freddy said. "He drummed that in my head."

So did Luke long ago. He told Freddy to always be ready to play. That evening Freddy played the Schumann and sent them whistling to Cairo. After three encores, all tangos, Freddy finally left the stage with tears in his eyes and his heart broken for having lost his second father.

Rufus was gone, and Rufus loved him. Freddy so wanted to believe that Gabrielle loved him, too, perhaps in her own way, and that she was smiling at him now as she stood next to Rufus. And then there was the beautiful Margo, who was a part of him forever. He needed her. It took a long time to realize it. And Marguerite needed her.

On the flight to Chicago no one spoke to Freddy and he was grateful. He looked out the window for a long time at the blue skies and the clouds below, thinking his life was a play of blue skies and clouds, starting on a black night in New Orleans when he was 10. The night his parents were killed.

"I've come to take you home to Chicago with me," Freddy's Uncle Dennis said later that day. "You'll go to school in Chicago and make lots of friends. Be anything you want when you grow up — doctor, scientist, astronaut, anything you set your mind to."

"I want to play music like my Daddy."

"Why on earth a musician, Freddy?"

"Because I feel music in my soul, Uncle Dennis."

"Big words, Freddy. You know what they mean?"

"I think so."

"Did that crazy brother of mine say that to you?"

"Don't you ever call my father crazy, Uncle Dennis, hear? My father wasn't crazy. He was a pianist like me."

"I'm sorry, son," Uncle Dennis said. "I didn't mean it to sound that way." He hugged Freddy. "Luke was my little brother. We disagreed on things. But I loved him."

"My Daddy said our music came from the heart and that we shared the same heart."

"Yes, Freddy, I see what you mean," Uncle Dennis said. "Then music it is. We'll bring Luke's piano to Chicago, too, so that you can play it."

Now Luke's piano was in Freddy's study in London. Flying to Chicago with a bank of memories, Freddy could almost hear Luke speaking to him from the piano, as he always did, and saying that he never thought of being anything else but a pianist.

The week Freddy took Rufus home from the hospital, they talked a lot about Luke and Connie. Rufus said Luke was explosive, but that all it took was one look from Connie and you could feel him mellowing like Tennessee whiskey. Then Connie sashayed over to Luke and he pulled his arms around her. That's all she did and he was peaceful like the heavens.

Sitting next to Rufus on the couch, Effie added, "Luke loved that girl. She was everything to him. She made his life magical."

"You have a lot of Luke in you, boy," Rufus said, nodding at Freddy and then at Effie. "But somewhere in the improvisation you lost your way."

"What would Luke have done in my place, Ruf?"

"Listen to me, boy," Rufus said, after taking time to consider his answer. "Stop thinking about what Luke would have done and start thinking what Freddy does. Let Luke go. If I knew my old friend, he would prefer Frederick Priestley making his own music."

"I think it's about time I did that, Ruf."

"I know your mama would have wanted that, honey," Effie followed. "She loved you oh so much, but she always knew you weren't meant to live in their shadow. They gave you wings, honey, so you keep on flying."

Looking out the window, Freddy realized that even though life took away a lot from him, it also gave him a lot. More than it gave a lot of other people. It was the way of things, his old friend Prince Hamid would probably say.

40

From the airport, Freddy drove straight to Effie's. He had already called her from Buenos Aires. He wrapped her in his arms and she cried for a long time. Without Rufus around, the house felt empty, as empty as Freddy's heart.

"Our Rufus is gone, Freddy honey," she murmured.

"I know he's gone, sweetheart, and we will miss him," Freddy said. "Yet Ruf would be the first to say not to use his memory to stop living." He took out his handkerchief and dried Effy's tears. "I'll take care of you. Margo and I will."

"But honey, you're young and you have your young family to think about."

"Effie, sweetheart, you're my family, too."

"Yes, we're family, aren't we, Freddy honey?" Effie stopped crying. "You're my boy."

"So, you will live with Margo and me. And the children."

"Oh honey, I couldn't leave this house," Effie protested. "Too many memories here. This was Ruf's house. His spirit's everywhere. I have my friends close by, and my church."

"We'll talk about that later, sweetheart," Freddy gave in. "For now, I want you to get dolled up and we'll go to Margo's for a family gathering."

They drove to Margo's house. Marguerite opened the door and jumped into Freddy's arms. "Oh, Daddy, I've been making chocolate chip cookies with Margo and Kristen and they're smashing." Marguerite then hugged Effie, who squeezed her and said, "Marguerite, honey, you give the sweetest hugs."

After speaking with Margo from Buenos Aires, Freddy called Nanny and instructed her to put Marguerite on the first flight to Chicago and that Margo and the children would pick her up from O'Hare.

Marguerite led Freddy and Effie into the kitchen and offered them each a cookie. Everyone waited for their response. Freddy pulled a fist, "Yes!" Effie beamed, "Oh honey, this is a lovely cookie." She hugged Margo and Kristen. Josh plowed into the kitchen and held out a hand to Freddy to shake. Freddy took it and then gave Josh a big hug. Josh gave Effie a hug, too.

Freddy turned to Margo. "Hello, beautiful."

"Hello yourself," she said.

Freddy kissed her forehead. "Will you marry me, sugar?" he asked, hugging her.

"I can't see a better ending to our story," she murmured.

"Or beginning," Freddy followed.

"Yes, both of them, my darling," Margo said, and kissed him. "The answer is yes."

The kitchen exploded in cheers and applause. More hugs followed.

Afterwards they all piled up in Freddy's rental and went out for spaghetti. Looking around the cavernous SUV, Margo wondered what happened to the Camaro.

"The Camaro's gone," Freddy said. "It was never the same after my sweet Aurore, anyway."

"It will never be the same in some things, my love."

"Just as well, Margo." Freddy took her hand and kissed it. It was warm and soft, just like her heart. "It's time to close the door on some things," he added.

"Well, this truck is a good start." Margo laughed.

"Yeah well, I asked the rental people to give me the biggest thing they had. I said I had an army to fit in it. So, they gave me Soldier Field on wheels."

Freddy watched Effie in the driver mirror. She seemed to be enjoying the kids and laughing with them. Yet he realized that Effie should live in her home, where she was comfortable, and where she spent years of happiness with the love of her life. He had promised Rufus to take care of her, and he would, he and Margo. Effie was family, after all.

At the small wedding ceremony a week later held at George Paulik's mansion, Freddy sat looking out the French window with Margo. It was a good spot to think about his life. He realized that even though he loved Margo since that party long ago, he fought needing her. Or needing anybody, in truth, because needing hurt. He needed Luke and Connie and, in the end, it blew up in his face and shattered his heart. It hurt a lot.

All that changed in Buenos Aires when he looked into the audience and saw Margo's image. She wore a big smile. He knew then that he planned to always look for her in the audience, if not in person, at least in spirit: to be there and to smile at him. He and Margo shared the same heart. It took two deaths to finally bring them together: Howard's and Gabrielle's. Why those two had to die for Freddy to have his Margo for the rest of his life he would never know. Only that it was a big price to pay for his happiness, and Margo's, but then he believed that life had its own way of setting prices.

Luke and Connie, his beloved parents, died when he was 10. All the love and all the talent in them gone in an instant. He then spent much of his life wondering why it happened to them.

"It's taken me all these years to finally accept their death," he told Margo earlier in the day. "Accept I must to live with myself and have a life with you, my children and the rest of my family."

After some discussion, they both agreed that Freddy should take Marguerite back to London to finish the school year before coming back home to Chicago. At the reception dinner, everyone else thought it a good idea. Turning to Paulik, Freddy said, "But then you've always known someday I would come home to Chicago."

"That would be true," Paulik said, and then nodding in Margo's direction, he added, "I'd be a fool not to come home."

"I only wish Ruf were here to see all this," Freddy lamented.

"He is, son," Paulik lifted his wine glass to toast. "Rufus would not miss your wedding, son."

"So then, Mister Paulik, what do you need me to do for the

conservatory?"

"Well, son, you belong out there on the concert stage, and in the recording studio. Show them what you've got."

"Ruf used to tell me that," Freddy recalled.

"I know, son," Paulik said. "Rufus and I knew each other better than you think. We were friends."

"And you both worked to make this moment possible."

"And that also be the truth, my boy."

"Mister Paulik, you're an old fox," Freddy said.

"Call me George, son," Paulik said with a smile. "Okay, then, spare a few moments for your alma mater when you have some down time."

"Professor Priestley," Phil snickered.

"God help us," Freddy snickered along.

After dinner, Marguerite asked Freddy to play something and he said he would if she joined him. He made room on the piano bench for her and began Schubert's song "The Trout" . . .

In einem Bachlein helle . . .

And Marguerite joined him . . .

Da schuss in froher Eil
Die launsche Forelle
Voruber wie ein Pfeil . . .

In the end, Marguerite threw her arms around Freddy's neck, beaming. "Oh, Daddy, that was splendid. We sent them whistling to Cairo, didn't we?

Freddy squeezed her in his arms. "We sure did, sugar."

"I love you, my beautiful Daddy."

"And I love you, my beautiful daughter."

Then they both rose and took a bow. Everyone gathered around the piano, still applauding.

"And now," Freddy announced, "I want to play something some-one dear to me composed a long time ago. She was a beautiful and passionate young girl who stole my heart with a single glance. It's a little love serenade for piano trio. I transcribed it for piano solo a long time ago, but never got the chance to play it. So here it is: *Serenade to Young Love* by Margo Kendrick Priestley.

The serenade rippled with youthful charm and romantic idealism.

It had Debussy's signature: lush and impressionistic. The opening allegro was like silky rain, young and fresh, the voice looking ahead, dreaming, expecting, hoping. In the second movement, the music slipped into an andante: tender and passionate, like love letters. The rondo finale burst into a glorious sunrise and turned boisterous like children at play.

In some way, Margo's music reflected his life, Freddy mused, starting with loving parents who opened the door to his musical dream. Although his journey took a bittersweet turn, in the end it brought him to this point surrounded by his family and friends.

From the piano, Freddy looked over at Margo and she placed her hand over her heart and mouthed silently, "I love you." And that's all Freddy needed to finally send himself whistling to Cairo.

BOOKS BY OBIE YADGAR

FICTION

    Whistling to Cairo
    Will's Music

NON-FICTION

    Obie's Opus

Ingram Content Group UK Ltd.
Milton Keynes UK
UKHW011305060623
422961UK00002B/232